Catch You Later, TRAITOR

Also by Avi

AVI

ALGONQUIN YOUNG READERS   2015

Published by
Algonquin Young Readers
an imprint of Algonquin Books of Chapel Hill
Post Office Box 2225
Chapel Hill, North Carolina 27515-2225

a division of
Workman Publishing
225 Varick Street
New York, New York 10014

LIBRARY OF CONGRESS CATALOGING-IN-PUBLICATION DATA
Avi, [date]
Catch you later, traitor : a novel / by Avi.—First edition.
pages cm
ISBN 978-1-61620-359-7
[1. Communism—Fiction. 2. Families—Fiction. 3. Brooklyn
(New York, N.Y.)—History—20th century—Fiction.] I. Title.
PZ7.A953Cat 2015
[Fic]—dc23   2014031983

10 9 8 7 6 5 4 3 2 1
First Edition

For Gary Schmidt

1

The way I see it, I stopped being a kid on April 12, 1951. We were playing our regular afternoon recess punchball game out in the schoolyard. I was about to smack the ball when Big Toby, who always played catcher, muttered, "Hey, Pete, that true about your parents?"

I looked over my shoulder. "What?"

"Is what Donavan said about your parents true?"

I stared at him as if he had walked off a flying saucer. Why would Mr. Donavan, our seventh-grade teacher, say anything about my parents? And how come I hadn't heard?

"Come on, Collison," Hank Sibley yelled at me. He was near second base, which was someone's sweater. "Stop gabbing. Recess almost up." He blew a huge bubble with his gum, which popped as I punched a shot inside third.

Kat, the only girl playing, raced home.

Our schoolyard was cement, which meant if you slid home, you'd peel off your skin. So no sliding allowed. Anyway, Kat stomped on her geography text, our home plate, and yelled "Dodgers win!" well before the ball was thrown home.

Grinning, I stood on first base, my English reader. Next moment the school bell clanged, so we grabbed our stuff and headed back to class.

"Kicky hit," Kat said to me.

Kat's real name was Katherine Boyer. Some people considered her a tomboy. I couldn't have cared less. She and I had been sitting next to each other ever since fourth grade. In fact, we did most things together: school, homework, movies, radio, and TV. Her mother once said we were back and forth between apartments so much, it was hard to know who lived where. Kat was pretty much the other half of my brain.

"Thanks," I said, but Big Toby's question—*"That true about your parents?"*—kept bouncing round my head like a steel marble in a lit-up pinball machine.

We poured into Brooklyn's Public School Number 10. The old brick building had no music room, no art room, no library, and no gym. All the same, it had a locker room stink.

Back at our wooden desks, all of them bolted to the floor, we did what we were supposed to do: sit with faces front, hands clasped, feet together, like rows of plaster ducks in a Coney Island shooting gallery. Since Donavan wasn't there, I wadded up a piece of paper and flicked it at Big Toby, hitting his fat neck.

He hooked a frown over his shoulder.

"Psst! What did Donavan say?"

The second I spoke, Donavan walked in. "No talking in class, Pete," he barked.

I ducked my head, looked toward Kat, and whispered: "Did Donavan say something about my parents yesterday?" It must have been when I'd left school early for a dentist drill.

She nicked a nervous nod.

That helped. "What'd he say?"

"Collison," said Donavan, "do I need to send you to the principal's office?"

Kat sneaked a small smile in my direction. It wasn't her usual smile. More like the smile on a store window mannequin: all show, no tell.

"Collison!" Donavan barked. "Eyes front."

With his potbelly, slack cheeks, large ears, and baggy eyes, Donavan reminded me of a beagle. He was strict, insisting we call him "Sir." His smiles were as rare as finding two bits on the sidewalk.

The way he told it, he was a World War Two vet with Technicolor tales about what happened to him and his buddies in the Pacific. In the mornings, when we stood by our desks, hands over hearts, pledging allegiance to the flag up front, he snapped a military salute sharp enough to chop cheap paper.

So when Donavan called you by your last name, it was like hearing a cop-car siren. You might not know what you were doing wrong but you stopped doing it. In other words, there was a smell in the air and it wasn't just the school.

School dragged on for another hour and a half, geography and then grammar. I was so rattled, my notion of a dangling participle was that long, skinny country of Chile.

When the class clock finally hit three and the bell rang, we poured out of school like beans from a split beanbag. It being Thursday afternoon, I should have gone to my once-a-week job, reading newspapers to a blind guy named Mr. Ordson, except he had called and canceled. Fine with me. I needed to talk to Kat about what Donavan said. But she raced ahead, and her mother was waiting for her outside.

Most times when Kat's mom saw me, she flashed a friendly "hello." That day when she saw me walking toward them, she hauled Kat away as if I had the chicken pox.

"Call me tonight!" I shouted to Kat.

With Kat gone, I searched for Big Toby, but he, too, had bolted. So there I was, alone, though what Toby said hung round like an annoying young cousin.

To calm myself down, I went over to Montvale Street to my favorite store, Ritman's Books.

When I walked in, Mr. Ritman, a little man with big Albert Einstein hair, was sitting behind the counter reading *Tales from the Crypt.*

Ritman always wore a green plastic visor that protected his eyes from the glare of the naked light bulb that dangled over his head like a cartoon idea. From his thin blue lips a lit cigarette hung, the burning end pointing down, the smoke drifting up, the ashtray in front of him a bird's nest built of butts. "'Lo, Pete," he mumbled, his eyes fixed on the gore in his comic book.

The front room of Ritman's store was filled with rotating wire racks stuffed with paperback books, comics, and magazines. I headed for the back room, which had the old detective magazines. I loved those mystery monthlies, ones like *Black Mask, Dime Detective,* and *Ellery Queen's Mystery Magazine.* Their covers always had some radioactive babe falling out of her dress next to a square-jawed guy about to either save her or kill her; it wasn't clear which. The stories were full of hard guys in hard situations with hard bad guys and dames, talking in such hard ways it would take a chisel to break their sentences apart.

My all-time favorite detective book was *The Maltese Falcon,* written by Dashiell Hammett. It was about Sam Spade, a hard-boiled private eye, a gumshoe, who was tough, honest, and stuffed with feelings, which he kept stuffed inside.

The Maltese Falcon starts something like this:

"There's a girl wants to see you, Sam.
Her name's Wonderly."
"A customer?"

"I guess so. You'll want to see her anyway: she's a knockout."
"Shoo her in, sweetheart," said Spade.
"Shoo her in."

Sam Spade, talking as if he were spitting firecrackers, was my Shakespeare. If I were a writer, that's the way I'd write. I was always trying to talk like him.

After reading *The Maltese Falcon* tons of times, listening to hours of mystery radio shows, and losing myself in detective stories, I knew what I wanted to be: a hard-boiled detective.

Trouble was, I had nothing to detect. And a detective with nothing to detect is like a fish living in a tree.

Anyway, I found an old *Black Mask* magazine, full of detective stories, the kind I loved. I flipped a dime to Ritman for the magazine and went to buy Ma her afternoon *Post* at the corner newsstand.

For a nickel, I got the newspaper and read the screaming headline:

PRESIDENT TRUMAN FIRES
GENERAL MACARTHUR!

I went to the back page.

BASEBALL SEASON ABOUT TO BEGIN
Yanks, Giants, Dodgers Hopes High

Thinking baseball until I turned onto my street, I tried to imagine the scene as if it were in a detective story I had written:

Hicks Street was lined with large apartment buildings with walls of blank-eyed windows, facing narrow streets with parked cars lined up like rows of dead sharks. Among the apartment buildings stood old brownstone houses, which seemed to have been assembled from slabs of brown bread. Here and there, skimpy pin oaks managed to grow in squares of unbreakable dirt. A tin sign that read "Curb Your Dog" was nailed to each oak. The cocker spaniel using the square closest to Pete Collison's building for a public squat must not have been able to read.

Pete shot through his building's lobby, grabbed two letters from the mail table—one for his parents, one for his brother Bobby—and took the elevator up to the third floor. Unlocking the door, he stepped into apartment 3B. As always, the place smelled like an unwashed ashtray and was as quiet as a sleeping brick.

I usually got home before my folks. Ma, a guidance counselor at Brooklyn Trinity School, often had to stay after school guiding kids. Dad was at New City College, where he taught American history. He got home around five. As for my brother Bobby—two years older than me—he usually stayed late at his high school working with his Rocket Club.

I headed down the dark, narrow hall, toward the

bedroom I shared with Bobby. The hall was lined with so many books it might as well have been a bargain basement bookstore. Small, framed family photographs of cousins, aunts, uncles, and grandparents were stuck between the books, creating the impression of a ship's passengers peeking at me through portholes.

I was halfway down the hall when our phone rang in the kitchen. Hoping it was Kat—we talked every day after school if we weren't together—I ran and picked up. "Hello?"

"Is this Pete?"

"Yeah."

"You need to help us, Pete."

"What? Who is this?"

The next sound was a dial tone that sang like a bee that hadn't bothered learning more than one note. I stood there, phone in hand, not sure if it had been a prank call or if someone had just threatened me.

Except . . . why would anyone threaten me?

Telling myself a threatening call was nuts, I dialed Kat. I wanted to tell her what had just happened, as well as ask about Donavan. There was no answer.

Leaving Ma's newspaper in the kitchen, I went to my room. A couple of years ago Dad had built a plywood partition down the middle of the room so Bobby and I could have our own space.

It was a gloomy room, the only outside light coming from the window over Pete's desk, which offered a terrific view of the building next door, maybe five feet away. The only slice of sunlight that managed to sneak in did so between eight and ten in the mornings. It didn't promise much and left early.

I dumped my schoolbag on my desk and tossed the *Black Mask* onto my bed, then glanced at the Dodger team picture and the pennant over my bed, thinking, *This year Brooklyn wins. No more "Wait till next year."* Then I settled in for some reading.

Didn't take too long before my stomach started asking for its after-school snack.

Back in the kitchen, I took out a box of Shredded Wheat and filled a bowl. Shredded Wheat wasn't my favorite cereal, but for three box tops, plus twenty-five cents, I could get a Secret Code Maker, which I could use to send and decode secret messages. Kat was working her way through boxes of Shredded Wheat, too, so we'd each have one.

I finished eating, ripped off the box top, collected the two other box tops from my room, and shook twenty-five cents from my Campbell's Mushroom Soup–can bank. Then I headed for Dad's small office to find an envelope and stamp.

Pete's ma claimed his dad's place was the biggest wastepaper basket in the universe. Papers were everywhere, some stacked, most not. Three walls of stuffed shelves had so many crisscrossing books, it looked like a massive game of pick-up sticks. Heaps of books covered the floor and topped the wooden file cabinets.

Next to the desk was a small table, which held an old Royal typewriter along with paper, regular and carbon for making copies. Over the desk was a picture of Thomas Jefferson, his white wig looking like a melting snowball.

Finding anything in Dad's office was hard. I searched his desktop and found nothing, but got lucky in the top desk drawer: an envelope alongside a small dish holding some three-cent stamps.

I was about to close the drawer when I noticed a photograph tucked under the dish, as if hidden. I pulled it out.

The faded black-and-white picture showed two girls, two boys, a man and a woman. I thought I recognized the woman as Dad's ma, Grandma Sally, when she was younger. The three kids were Dad and his two older sisters. I didn't recognize the other, younger boy. One of Dad's friends, I guessed. As for the man, he looked like Chris, Dad's uncle.

But—how come I hadn't seen the photo before? Ma stuck family pics all over the apartment, and she was forever working on her photo scrapbooks. The point is, Dad never was interested in family photos. How come he had this picture in his desk?

I did what a detective would do: I rummaged through the drawer for other photos. When I didn't find any, I tucked that one photo back exactly where I found it, then went to mail my envelope in the corner mailbox. As I walked, I kept mulling over the phone call and that picture. None of my mulls mounted to more than molehills.

Back in my room, I flopped on my bed and went back to my *Black Mask* magazine and that story I'd started, "The False Burton Combs." It was about a detective who pretended to be someone else so he could catch some crooks as he tried to keep from being murdered himself.

I was still reading when I heard the front door open. I quickly put the book over my face, as if I'd fallen asleep, so I could do some detective listening.

Ma—the click of her heels told me it was her—came in first, stood at my doorway, probably looked in, then went down the hall toward the kitchen. Dad, with his slower, heavier step, came next. Bobby was last. Always in a hurry, he burst into our room with enough clatter to wake me, if I really had been asleep. I just lay there.

Then, when he left the room, I worked on dinner smells. I detected fried liver, onions and beans, plus spinach, Dad's favorites.

Around six we had family dinner. I had been right about the menu. The routine was the same as every night. Ma sat at one end of the table, near the stove. Dad was at the other end, Bobby and I in the middle. Ma always served Dad first, then us kids, herself last.

Ma said, "How was school?"

I was about to tell my folks about the phone call when Bobby said, "I got big news in the mail."

Far as I was concerned, Bobby was mostly a germ, so most times I didn't listen to him. This time I did. Seems the National Advisory Committee for Aeronautics, a government agency, ran a summer camp for smart high school kids. Bobby applied, and had been accepted.

"You'll see," he said, "I'm going to do so well at this camp, I'll get into a great college. A great college will get me into the U.S. rocket program. The rocket program will put me on the moon." His grin told us he was already doing cartwheels up there.

I didn't cheer the way my folks did, but I wasn't going to rain on his party, either.

After dinner, my folks went into the radio room to talk about how General MacArthur had been fired by President Truman. These days all they talked about was the war in Korea, Communism, Republicans, and Democrats. I stayed in the kitchen, glad it was my night to do cleanup.

After a while Kat called to go over geography, but she was so rushed I couldn't get in a word to ask about Donavan. In fact, she jumped off the phone so fast I wondered why. Not her normal way. One more riddle.

At seven thirty, I listened to *Martin Kane, Private Eye* on the Mutual Broadcasting System. Then I went back to "The False Burton Combs." I couldn't concentrate, too distracted by the day's strange events: Big Toby's remark, how Donavan was treating me, Kat not telling me what Donavan said, her mother dragging her away without a spot of smile, that mysterious phone call, the photograph in my dad's desk, and finally Kat's rushed call.

Here was my chance. In fact, plenty of chances: If I wanted to figure things out, I should keep acting like a detective. Keep my eyes and ears open. Find clues. Try to connect the day's dots.

I couldn't connect those dots. Not yet. But by the next day, so much happened, all I could *see* was dots.

It was Friday the Thirteenth and that should have been
warning enough. It started regular, with me waiting in
front of my apartment building for Kat. I reminded myself that I was going to do Sam Spade that day: be calm,
watchful, and collect facts. First job: get Kat to tell me what
Donavan had said.

She came running, her denim Eisenhower jacket un-
buttoned, her tin Nancy Drew lunch box in one hand,
her fringed cowgirl book satchel in the other. Kat couldn't
decide which she wanted to be, Roy Rogers's wife, cowgirl
Dale Evans, with her trusty buckskin horse, Buttermilk, or
Nancy Drew, the girl detective with her own blue roadster.

I liked her all ways.

She was taller than me by a head, with brown hair cut pageboy style with bangs. Her eyes were brown, she had a pug nose, and she wore cheaters (rimless glasses) too big for her round face. She looked like a skinny owl that hadn't grown into her eyes.

While most girls in our class wore white cotton shirts and skirts, Kat wore flannel plaid shirts and jeans, the shirts never tucked in, the jeans always baggy. Her Wingfoot sneakers were forever smudged. The way she dressed left her parents frosted. I thought she looked cool.

Soon as she reached me, she started gabbing about the *Roy Rogers* TV episode she'd seen the night before. Providing every detail, she never stopped. It was as if she didn't want me to talk.

Only when she took a breath could I slip in my first detective question. "Hey," I said, "the other day, when I left school to go to the dentist, what did Donavan say about my parents?"

Not only did Kat not answer, she walked faster.

"Hey! What did he say?" I pressed.

She shoved her glasses up and took a few seconds to say, "Not much."

"How come you didn't tell me?"

Her face flashed something I'd never seen from her before: fright. Before I could take it in, she turned away and said, "I forget."

I wanted to say, "How could you forget?" but didn't. I told myself to stay cool, detective style. I got the message.

Something was wrong. So I backed off. I'd try for more information later. In the meantime, I told her something I knew she'd like. "Sent in for my Code Maker."

That got a smile. "I've got half a box of Shredded Wheat to go," she said, only to turn on the no-talk switch again.

After a moment, I said, "Baseball season starts Tuesday."

"We'll beat the Giants easy this year," she said.

"Won't even take it easy," I agreed, and we talked Dodgers the rest of the way.

If you lived in Brooklyn—and most everybody I knew did—your blood was Brooklyn Dodger blue. Didn't matter what else was going on, even if there had been a hurricane or a blizzard, you talked Dodgers, you thought Dodgers, you breathed Dodgers, and you hated the New York Giants.

Life was that simple.

We got to school just as the eight thirty bell rang. In class, with Donavan up front doing his military salute and our hands on hearts, we pledged allegiance to the flag, squeezing the whole thing into one long word.

Then Donavan said, "Any announcements?"

Chuck Guterson raised his hand.

"Yes, Chuck?"

"Mr. Donavan, sir, baseball begins next week."

Donavan said, "It sure does. Who's going to win the pennant this year?"

The whole class, including me, yelled, "Dodgers!"

"Who's going to lose?"

"Giants!" we roared, and banged our desktops.

For once, Donavan laughed. "Well, keep your fingers crossed. And remember, Dodger rally on Monday. Wear something blue."

I couldn't wait, though I needed to figure out what I'd wear.

"Also," said Donavan, "the other day I forgot to say I was disappointed that only half of your parents came to Parents' Night."

Typical Donavan. One second, he had the class dancing with Dodger talk. Next second, he turned everything frigid with his Parents' Night thing.

Still, my dad had gone, so I felt okay.

Donavan remained before his desk, as if making a decision. Then he said, "When we did the Pledge of Allegiance this morning I was reminded that I needed to say something important." He looked right at me. "I spoke about it Wednesday but Pete wasn't here. Please pay close attention."

I sat up straight, eyes locked front.

"Starting today we're going to be studying our 1846 war with Mexico. As we all know, the United States is at war in Korea. This time we are fighting Communism, the Reds being our greatest enemy. We also know—or should know—Reds have infiltrated our government, even our schools."

Donavan looked right at me. "Pete, can you tell the class what Communism is?"

Taken by surprise and pointing to myself to be sure, I said, "Me?"

"Yes, you."

Why was he asking me? I had no idea how to answer. To make things worse, the whole class was looking at me with Orphan Annie eyes.

"Come on, Pete," Donavan pushed. "Tell us what you know about Communism."

"I . . . I think . . . it's the . . . the kind of government the Soviet Union has. Which is against us, I guess."

"You *guess*," said Donavan, his sarcasm dripping like ice cream in August.

He picked up the big blue dictionary sitting on his desk. "Come on up here, Pete."

I found my feet and went up front.

Donavan handed me the book. "Please open at the marker."

I opened the book where a red ribbon was sticking out and looked to Donavan for directions.

"I've marked a word and definition. Please read."

There was a black line next to the word *Communism*. I hesitated.

"Read it," he insisted.

Because of all the big words, and being uncomfortable, nervous even, I read clumsily. " 'Communism. A system of social organization in which all economic and social activity is controlled by a totalitarian state denominated by a single political party.' "

I looked at Donavan.

"What do you make of that?" he asked.

"I . . . don't know . . ."

"You don't *know?*"

"I mean . . . I don't know what total—totalitarian means."

"Then look it up."

Fumbling, I found the word and glanced at Donavan again.

"Read it," he said.

I sucked up spit to wet my mouth, and read: " 'Totalitarian. A centralized government that does not tolerate parties of differing opinions and that exercises dictatorial control over many aspects of life.' "

"Now what do you think?"

"It's . . . not good."

"Not good," echoed Donavan, saying "good" so it sounded bad. There were some giggles from my classmates. Hoping for a friendly look, I peeled a peek at Kat, but she was staring down at her desk.

"Fortunately," Donavan went on, "there are people in government, the Congress, the FBI—I have FBI friends—who are ferreting out red traitors, people who pretend to like America but secretly oppose it. All of us, even kids like you, need to do your patriotic duty to make sure reds, Commie symps, fellow travelers, and pinkos, un-Americans, don't infiltrate our lives. None of us should have anything to do with reds."

Donavan had shot speeches like that before. This time he was aiming it right at me. I felt like enemy number one without knowing my crime.

Most of the kids sat stony silent, and Big Toby and Sibley were glaring at me. Kat was still staring at her desk.

Donavan went on, "So when we study history, especially American history, we need to be alert to Commie lies." He gave me a furious look, and then turned to the class. "Let's have no mollycoddling of reds in this classroom. Do we all understand that?"

"Yes, sir," the class chorused.

Donavan came back to me: "Red traitors should be put in jail or kicked out of the country. Love it or leave it. I hope you all believe that."

Red traitors? How come he was marking me when he said that?

"Take your seat, Pete."

Twenty pairs of eyes followed me back to my desk. If Donavan had put a dunce cap on me, I couldn't have felt more humiliated.

I sat down and glanced at Kat. She was squashed down so low it was as if she was being swallowed by her desk.

"Okay," said Donavan, "history."

Glad to be no longer the center of attention, I pulled out my history book.

Donavan started talking about the Mexican war. "Who was the American president during this war?"

Now, my father didn't just teach college students

American history; he loved teaching us at home, too. If there was one subject I knew, it was that. So I raised my hand to tell him the answer to his question was President Polk. In fact, I waved my hand as if I was drowning. Though no one else lifted a hand, Donavan didn't call on me.

As class continued, he threw out more questions, like who was the big U.S. general during the war. I knew that one, too: Zachary Taylor. In fact, I knew the answers to *all* his questions. Donavan never called on me.

Finally, the bell rang. "Recess," Donavan announced.

I sat there trying to figure out why Donavan was treating me the way he did. I tried to think what Sam Spade would have done. The best I could come up with was, ask Donavan.

I wasn't sure what would happen. Just knew I had to.

As usual, the punchball guys and Kat hauled on jackets and sweaters and began picking teams as they headed out. I hung back and went to Donavan's desk, where he was going through his lesson book.

"Yes, Pete?" he said without looking up or stopping his work.

"Mr. Donavan, sir, can I ask a question?"

"It's still a free country."

"Sir, I knew the answers to those history questions you were asking. But you never called on me. Not even when I was the only one with my hand up. I mean . . . how come?"

Donavan gave me a look with a face that suggested I'd insulted his mother.

"Pete," he said, "I hope you heard me when I spoke at the beginning of history class."

"Yes, sir."

"Then you heard me say I wasn't going to mollycoddle any reds or pinkos in my class."

"Yes, sir. Only . . . what's that have to do with me? I'm not a pinko or a red."

"A pinko is a Commie sympathizer. Though you pretend otherwise, I think you know all about Commies, Pete."

"I *do*?"

His face turned uglier. "Pete, I don't intend to allow any Red propaganda in my class. Propaganda which I doubt you even understand."

"Sir," I said, "are you saying I'm . . . a Commie?"

"Your father sure talked like one at the parents' meeting. And what parents do, their kids are. I hope I've made myself clear. Go take your recess, Collison." He dove back into his work.

I stood there, feeling like a skunk who had wandered into a perfume shop. Then, as I walked down to the schoolyard, I tried to untangle Donavan's words. Dad? A Communist? What was he talking about?

By the time I got outside, the guys and Kat were already playing punchball. Seeing six on the field, seven at bat, I started for the outfield.

"Time out!" shouted Sibley. "Hey, Collison. Hold it."

I stopped. "What?"

"Commies can't play."

"Huh?"

"You heard what Donavan said. We just had a meeting and made a rule: No Commies can play."

"What are you talking about? I'm not a Commie."

"Donavan said so," called Parker.

"Yeah," shouted Big Toby. "And we're having nothing to do with traitors."

"Right," added Corelli. "No reds infiltrating us."

Kat was playing first base. I threw a look at her. She didn't throw it back. The others were glaring at me as if I was a mound of hot horse manure.

I tried to think of a smart comeback. I couldn't.

"So beat it, Collison," called Sibley, and blew one of his large gum bubbles. The schoolyard was 4 a.m. quiet, until Sibley's bubble burst with a bang!

I turned to Kat one last time. I don't know what she was looking at. It wasn't me.

Ever been in a bathtub after the hot water has drained out? Suddenly you're freezing, and naked. That's the way I felt for the rest of the day. But did I understand what was happening? No.

When three o'clock came, I waited for Kat outside the classroom. She shot by me so fast I had to run after her.

"Hey, Kat! Wait up. Where you going?"

Without stopping, she called over her shoulder, "Have to meet my parents. We're going upstate to visit my aunt."

"The whole weekend?"

"Uh-huh."

"Right away?"

She rushed on.

"Kat!" I bellowed. "What's going on?"

She stopped. "I can't be late," she called, and fled.

I was still standing there when two guys from my class, David Johnson and Joel Toliver, slammed me with their shoulders as they passed.

"Commie," muttered David.

Shaken by more than the shoulder shoves, I left school by the back door, probably the first time I ever did that.

I walked home feeling as mixed up as a thousand-piece jigsaw puzzle dumped on a table. I didn't even know what the picture was supposed to be. I wasn't stupid. I knew some stuff about Communism. Those days, grown-ups talked about it a lot. The Soviet Union was our enemy. So was red China. We were fighting a war in Korea against reds—China and North Korea. At the dinner table over the last few weeks, I heard my folks talking about how U.S. Communists had to register with our government. How the Rosenbergs, a husband and wife, had been sentenced to death for being Soviet spies. How some writer told something called the Un-American Activities Committee that a whole lot of Hollywood directors and writers were Communists.

I heard my parents talk about those things, but for me it was like alphabet soup. I knew the letters but I swallowed them whole, without making words or sentences with them.

So, other than knowing that Communism was bad,

that it was the opposite of America, I didn't really know much else. Now Donavan said I was a Commie because my dad was one. For starters, I knew that was dead wrong. Dad was always talking up America to us, how great and important it was. Absolutely, he wasn't a Red. And anyway, if he *was* a Red, did that make me one?

I was so lost in my thoughts, it took me a while to notice a man walking half a block behind me. I didn't pay much attention at first. It was only when I checked a third and fourth time and the guy was still there that I began to be bothered.

I did some detective tricks to see if he was really following me: I slowed down, and he slowed down. I went fast. He went fast. He must have wanted me to know I was being shadowed, because he was so obvious about it. What was going on?

Wanting to act natural, I bought Ma's afternoon paper and then headed into our building, checking that man one last time. He looked regular, not too young, not too old, wearing a dark overcoat and a fedora. Mr. Ordinary.

As soon as I got into our apartment, the phone rang. I wasn't sure I wanted to answer.

It kept ringing.

Half curious, half nervous, I went to the kitchen and picked up. "Hello?"

"This Pete?" It sounded like the man from the day before.

I said, "Who's this?"

"Are you going to work with us, Pete?"

"What are you talking about?"

He hung up.

I bolted into my parents' bedroom, cracked the Venetian blinds, and peeked down to the street. On the corner was a red telephone booth. Stepping out was the same guy who had been following me. Who was he? How was I supposed to work with him? On what? Why did he hang up if he wanted something from me?

I went to my room and dropped onto the bed, wishing Kat was around. As I sat there, it popped into my head that maybe she was around, that she didn't want to speak to me, that her saying she was going away was a way to avoid me, the way she did at school.

I called her. When no one answered, I felt better. But it's bad news when the only good news is that nothing worse happens.

I sat at the kitchen table struggling to figure things out. As I sat there, I noticed the headlines in the paper I bought for Ma.

SUBVERSIVE ACTIVITIES CONTROL BOARD TO HOLD HEARINGS

Representative Kierman announced that his Congressional subcommittee will soon be holding hearings in New York City respecting the counterattack by the Communist conspiracy in the United States against the government's programs to expose Communist operations.

I read the article a few times but didn't see anything connected to my parents—or me. Then I thought about the definitions Donavan made me read in class. I didn't see any connections to my father there either. As for "dictatorial control," the only one who tried that was my older brother.

I recalled what Donavan said: Commies were people who pretend to like America, but secretly oppose it.

All of a sudden, I asked myself a whole new question . . . What if my parents *were* Commies—*secret* Commies?

I spent the afternoon thinking like a detective, wanting to figure out how to solve all these mysteries.

That's why, when Ma stuck her head in my room around four thirty and said, "Hi, honey. Have a good day?" I just said, "Okay," and considered her in mystery style:

Mrs. Collison was a short, plump lady who often said she weighed too much. Pete had a rule: Never argue with a lady about her weight. With dark hair framing a round, dimpled face, a face usually full of smiles, she didn't seem like Commie material, no more than a house cat might be a lion in disguise.

I was pleased with my description—and had ruled out Ma being a Commie—until I remembered a picture I saw of that Rosenberg woman—the convicted Commie spy. She was short and dumpy, but they said they were going to put her in the electric chair.

Then Pete reminded himself: dames are full of surprises.

Ma smiled. "Are you looking forward to the weekend?"
"Sure."
"What are you and Kat planning?"
"She and her parents went somewhere for the weekend."
"Oh, that's too bad."
I shrugged.
"Dinner in thirty minutes."
I picked up *Black Mask* and read "Five O'Clock Menace" until my brother Bobby showed up. I looked at him, too, detective style:

If there was one member of the Collison family who was traitor material, it would have been Bobby, Pete's older brother. With his lean, tense face, Bobby worked hard not to smile. An ace in school, he'd convinced his friends he was a genius. The problem was, he believed it, too. Bobby also liked to seem mysterious, but Pete knew that, deep inside, Bobby was a bore.

Bobby flung his schoolbooks and leather flight jacket onto his bed, and said, "What are you doing?"

"Nothing."

"As usual," he sneered. Before I could think of a come-back, he went out.

Dad was the last to come home.

Professor Dennis Collison had a schedule as regular as the rising of the sun. He left his office at four fifteen, took the subway, and arrived home around five. For the past few weeks, he had stayed later on Wednesdays to meet with evening students who dropped by his office.

Mostly bald, he blamed his condition on the army hel-met he had kept on for four years. He did have a fringe of gray hair, and a bristly black mustache that made him look like a smiling walrus.

The way to describe Professor Collison was "mild." As for being a Commie, about to overthrow the country, he didn't have the strength to flip a flea. A war wound had given him a stiff and slightly twisted right arm. The most athletic things he did were play checkers with his younger son and talk baseball.

Standing in the doorway to my room, Dad said, "Hey, Pal, have a good day?"

"Sure," I said, getting good at lying. "You?"

"A little too long. We listening to Sam Spade tonight?"

"Hope so."

After Dad left, I studied the picture of him in his 1941 army uniform that I'd stuck on my wall. I also had his dog tags as well as the Purple Heart he got when he'd been wounded in Germany in 'forty-five.

"Dinner!" Ma called.

As I headed to the kitchen, I knew I had to make a decision: Was I going to tell my parents about Donavan, and what happened in school, the phone calls, Kat? About that picture in Dad's desk?

A quick question: What would Sam Spade do? He'd poke around looking for clues, watching, listening, and waiting. But he'd keep everything he learned in his fists until he put it all together. Then he'd gather the suspects in the case, fling out the truth like a stick of dynamite, and *Boom!*—case solved!

One other thing: Spade always worked alone. The only person he sometimes talked to was his secretary, Effie, the one he called "sweetheart." Of course, she wasn't his girlfriend. More like Kat and me, best friends.

So I decided to work on my own and keep my mouth shut until I figured the facts.

During dinner, Bobby kept going on about his science camp. While he jabbered, I studied my parents. Were they Communists? It seemed impossible, but I reminded myself that private eyes uncovered hidden truth. Hidden, like five feet deep.

At eight, when it was time for *The Adventures of Sam Spade, Detective,* I told myself I needed to pay special attention. It would be like taking lessons from the best.

I set the radio dial for 660, WNBC, and thought about where I was.

The Collisons' radio room was small, with two soft couches meeting at right angles, like marshmallows stuck together. In front of them was a rag rug, on which stood a low table with a dirty ashtray. The shelves on two walls were full of books and record albums, though one shelf was reserved for games: a checkers set, Monopoly, and Clue. Against another wall stood a Philco cabinet radio with a record player and changer. Above it was a photo of the whole Collison family from last Christmas. In short, the room was like ten million other rooms, not the kind of place a decent clue would want to call home.

With me on one couch and Dad on the other, we settled into listening to "The String of Death Caper."

It was about identical twins, brothers, one good, the other bad, one left-handed, the other right-handed. The good one was a bank teller. The bad one killed his brother and took his place in the bank, so he could rob it. How did Spade figure things out? Seems left-handed and right-handed people tie string knots opposite ways. The way the bad brother tied up the packs of stolen money gave him away. Case solved.

When the show ended, I turned the radio off. "Wish they hadn't got rid of that Duff actor," I said. "He was a better Spade."

Dad said, "I'm afraid Duff was blacklisted."

"What's that?"

"People won't hire him."

"Why not?"

"He was accused of being a Communist."

More Communists! "Is he one?"

"I have no idea. But I'm afraid there's more bad news. The show is going off the air in two weeks. It's been canceled."

"You kidding?"

"Nope. The writer who invented Sam Spade, a guy named Dashiell Hammett, has been accused of being a Red, too. Like Duff."

I grabbed my chance. "Dad," I said, "what do you think of all this Red business?"

Dad sat for a minute, then reached into a pocket, pulled out some loose change, and handed me a Roosevelt dime. "Have you ever looked closely at one of these?"

"No. Why should I?"

"It seems that the artist, somebody named John Sinnock, who made the engraving of the president, put his initials on it. Can you see them?"

I squinted at the dime but didn't see a thing.

"Look under Roosevelt's neck." He pointed to a spot on the coin. "Right there."

That time I saw the little letters.

Dad said, "Some people think that those letters, *J* and *S*, stand for 'Joseph Stalin.'"

"The Soviet dictator?"

He nodded. "Those people believe the dime is a Communist plot."

I stared at the coin, then back at Dad. "That true?"

Dad got up. "These are strange times, Pete," was the only answer he gave. "Keep the change. I need to talk to your ma."

I took the dime into my room, put it under my lamp, and stared at the tiny J.S. under the president's neck. They were there, all right. In other words, if you look hard enough you can see things. Sam Spade couldn't have said it better.

Then it hit me. I had asked Dad what he thought of all this Red business. He hadn't answered my question. How come?

After breakfast on Saturday, Bobby announced he was meeting with his high school Rocket Club. "I'm out of here," he called, and slammed the door.

My folks got ready for their weekly grocery shopping. To me Ma said, "Going to the movies?"

Most Saturday mornings, Kat and I went to the neighborhood theater for a kids' movie show. For twenty-five cents, you could see seven cartoons, a *March of Time* newsreel, and a full-length flick. It was like starting your day with dessert. That week they had an old detective movie, *Bulldog Drummond Strikes Back*. I really wanted to see it, even though it wouldn't be the same without Kat.

Dad said, "Don't forget to lock the door when you go out."

"It's supposed to rain," Ma added as they left.

As I set off for the theater, the sky was ash gray. If my mood had had a color, it would have matched. I checked around a couple of times to see if I was being followed. I didn't see anyone. Ease up, I told myself. Bad things don't happen in the morning: It's Saturday night when the bad stuff hits.

When I reached the movie theater, dozens of kids— laughing, yelling, fooling, and having a grand time—were on line. They kept coming, too, from all over Brooklyn. The only adults in sight were the ones taking money for tickets, candy, and popcorn.

Without Kat, I wasn't sure who I'd sit with. Then I saw Big Toby, Phil Corelli, and Hank Sibley.

I hesitated before going over to them, wondering if the school Commie stuff would start again. I decided I'd act as if nothing had happened.

They had been horsing around. Soon as I showed, it was as if someone pulled hard on their reins.

Sibley gave me a look as sweet as a dirty dishrag. "What are you doing here?"

"What do you think? Going to the movies."

"No Commies allowed," Big Toby said.

With my mouth feeling like it was full of stale crackers, I said, "What are you talking about? I'm not a Commie."

Other kids started looking around.

Toby shoved me toward the curb, saying, "No reds allowed."

I said, "It's a free country. I can go to the movies."

"You want to eat a knuckle sandwich, Commie?" Big Toby stood there, double fisted, daring me to fight.

Wobbly with anger, I made my own fists. "I'm not a Commie. I can do what I want."

Toby backed off.

After one last glare at him, I went to the end of the line, where I didn't know anyone.

It wasn't cold, but Pete shivered. When it started to rain, he felt like the last soggy cornflake in the bowl.

The box office opened. Kids surged forward, Pete swept along with them. Inside, the theater was a zoo without bars. Kids were crawling over seats, running up and down aisles, shouting, throwing popcorn and candy wrappers on the floor. An old lady with a flashlight raced around, trying to keep order. She did no better than a bottle cap on a volcano. It was a regular Saturday at the movies.

Finding a seat in a back row, I shrank small and tried to think big about ways to get back at my classmates. I couldn't come up with anything. All I could do was mutter, "I'm not a Red."

I was glad when the lights dimmed.

There were huge cheers when the first cartoon, a Tom and Jerry, began. It was the usual: Tom the cat (large and dumb) constantly tried to catch Jerry the mouse (small and smart). Though Tom invented wild ways to slam the mouse, he always lost and ended up getting slammed himself.

At first, it was funny, but then I began to feel sorry for Tom, who was always being beat up. I felt like him. Was him. When Tom was flattened dollar-thin by a steamroller that came from nowhere, I jumped up and tore out of the theater.

Outside, the rain was pounding. I ran, fighting tears and the downpour. I lost both fights.

I raced home, slammed the door shut, and locked it as if Jerry the mouse was at my heels. Breathless and shaky, I stood in the empty hallway. Ma and Dad were still out.

I changed into dry duds, then went to the kitchen, slotted up some toast, and laid out a big sandwich. I was still eating when the doorbell rang. My first thought was, *Kat's back*. I ran down the hallway and yanked the door open.

Instead of Kat, a man was standing there. His face was young and smooth, his hair short and blond, blue eyes and a sharp chin. Under his open, wet raincoat, he wore a brown suit, white shirt, and green tie. In his hands, he held a hat. He looked at me, and smiled nicely.

"Hi," he said. "My name is Tom Ewing. I'm from the Federal Bureau of Investigation. The FBI."

The FBI.

My jaw opened so wide you could have driven in a Cadillac. Then I realized he was the guy who had followed me the other day.

He said, "This is Mr. Dennis Collison's home, isn't it?"

"Yes . . . sir."

"May I come in?"

"Who . . . who'd you say you were?" I had heard him. I just didn't want to have heard.

Keeping his smile in place, he whipped out a wallet and flipped it open like a cowboy pulling out his six-shooter. There it was: a card with his picture on it and the letters *F, B, I,* big and bold.

"Are you Pete?" he asked.

I nodded.

"And your father is Dennis Collison, correct?"

I gave a dumb nod.

"You look like him."

"You know him?"

"Of course."

"How?"

"It's my job to investigate people like him."

His words sent an ice cube sliding down my back and into my drawers.

"May I come in?"

"What . . . do you want?" I said. I wished he'd go away but didn't know how to make it happen.

"I'd like to talk to your father."

"He's not here."

"How about your mother?"

"Not here either."

"Your brother?"

"No."

"Ah," he said, his smile as real as a three-dollar bill. "Well, you could talk to me."

"What about?"

"Lots of things. May I come in?"

"I . . . I don't think so."

"Hey, Pete, there's no reason to be frightened of me. I'm a nice guy. I have a kid brother your age. In seventh grade, too."

He seemed to know about me.

"Do you work hard in school, Pete?"

"Sort of."

"Which New York team do you root for?"

"Dodgers."

"I'm for Cincinnati."

"The Reds?"

"Cincinnati," he said, frowning.

Though I felt he was toying with me, the best I could do was hope my parents got home.

"Are you going to let me in, Pete?"

I shook my head.

"How come?"

"I'm not supposed to let strangers in."

"That's smart. But I was hoping you would consider me a friend. Here." He took out his wallet again and handed me a card. "My personal card. You can call me any time."

I took it without looking at it.

"You're not worried because I'm from the FBI, are you?"

My head shook the lie.

With his smile fixed, and his blue-eyed gaze as sharp as a drill, I felt as if he were attempting to unnerve me. I hoped he couldn't tell my heart was working like a baby's rattle.

Then he said, "Or maybe you're worried because there's some secret you're hiding."

"Huh?"

"Maybe a picture of Stalin in your living room?"

"Stalin?" I echoed dumbly.

"Yeah, you know, the Soviet dictator. The guy who wants to destroy America. Do you ever talk politics with your dad?"

I couldn't believe what he was saying.

"You know, Pete, you could help your father a lot."

I just looked at him.

"We know he was a member of the Communist Party."

Pow! It was as if the world's heavyweight champ, Jersey Joe Walcott, had landed a glove on my chin.

"If you cooperated with us," he went on, "things could go a lot easier for him, and for your whole family. You know anything about your grandfather?"

I felt as if he was throwing punches at me from all sides. All I could do was cover up by being silent.

He said, "You love your country, don't you, Pete?"

I think I nodded.

He tapped a finger on my chest. I flinched. "If you love America," he said, "then work for and with America. If you have no secrets to hide, don't hide them. I really think you need to help us, Pete."

That's what the voice on the phone said.

"I'm guessing you don't feel like talking," he went on. "But I'll be honest with you. We'd like to know a whole lot more about your father's family. So I need you to tell your dad I was here. Okay? Here's an extra card. You can have one. Make sure you give him the other."

I remained standing, struggling to breathe, unable to speak.

He took a step back. "Nice talking to you, Pete. In fact, why don't you come by my office sometime?" He nodded toward the cards in my hand. "You have my address there. We could talk some more. Now remember, tell your dad I was here." He held out his hand. I shook it. He had a grip like Superman.

He strode down the hall only to swing around just before the elevator. "Hey, I'm good friends with someone you know. Bet you can't guess who."

I shook my head.

"Your teacher. Ricky Donavan."

That was the knockout punch.

I flung myself against the door and locked and chained it. Then I tore to my parents' bedroom, pried open the Venetian blinds, and stole a look down to the street. Ewing walked out of the building and into a small black Ford and drove away. I did get a view of the license plate: New York, PED459.

Trying to understand what had just happened, I kept staring down.

If Noah wanted to make a comeback, this was his day. A storm was sweeping the streets, making the surface glisten like an oil slick. Puddles were turning into pools. Cars, lights on, wipers whipping, rolled by with wet hisses. A lady in a green rubber raincoat hurried along, yanking a white Scottie that was finding the wet pavement more interesting than she was. Everything was ordinary, except Pete's head, which was spinning like a merry-go-round that wasn't merry.

"We know he was a member of the Communist Party. If you cooperated with us, things could go a lot easier for him."

What did he mean? My dad a Communist? I didn't believe it. How could I cooperate? If I didn't, would Ewing arrest Dad? Me?

"Know anything about your grandfather?"

What was there to know about my grandfather? Nobody talked about him. Not even Dad. Or Grandma Sally. He died before I was born. I didn't even know his name.

I went into the radio room and stared at that family picture. In it, gathered round Grandma Sally, were Ma, Dad, me, Bobby, my uncles and aunts, my dad's uncle, my cousins. Little guys down front, littlest in my aunt's arms.

The most normal family in the world.

Except, maybe it wasn't. All I knew was that the world I knew had stopped being the world I knew.

I went back to my room and studied the cards Ewing gave me.

I needed to calm down and think it through. Try to look at the pieces like a detective.

Ewing came when I was alone. I was sure that was no accident. He had followed me from school the other day. He was watching me. But it wasn't me they were after, it was Dad. *"Tell your dad I was here."*

Ewing must have come because Donavan told him Dad was a Communist.

That's why I made the big decision that I would *not* tell Dad about Donavan and school. Which meant nothing about the FBI, either. On my own, I'd find the truth about Dad, that he wasn't a Communist. I'd take the facts to Ewing and make him leave Dad alone. That would make Donavan look stupid.

That decision made me feel strong, and tough. I was still sitting there telling myself that I was strong when I heard someone straining to get the door open. My toughness turned to tissue.

I jumped up, rammed Ewing's cards into my pocket, and crept toward the door. Was the FBI back? Were they breaking in so they could arrest me? My dad?

With my heart doing backflips, I called, "Who . . . who is it?"

"Pete! Unlatch the chain."

My father's voice.

With relief, I cried, "Wait a second."

I undid the chain and yanked the door open. My parents stood there, dripping wet, their full paper grocery bags all but bursting.

Ma said, "Goodness, Pete, why was the chain on?"

Right then I could have told them about the FBI guy. I didn't. I had made my decision. I threw a shrug and mumbled, "Don't know."

"I thought you were going to the movies," Dad said.

"The rain," I said.

Ma laughed. "Afraid you'd melt?"

"I guess." To keep from talking, I grabbed a couple of their bags, went into the kitchen, and helped them put food away. Dad lit a cigarette and started to make coffee. I watched him. Could he really be a Communist?

Ma got on the phone for her weekly long-distance call to her mother in Indiana. I went to my room and hid the two FBI cards in my *Black Mask*.

Sitting at my desk, I kept thinking about Dad, trying to remember things he had said, political things. When he talked about politics, he talked about history. And rights.

Rights for Negroes. Rights for women. Unions. Sure, there was talk about Communism. But actually, as I thought about it, it was mostly *anti*-Communism he and Ma spoke about. In the end, I decided that Dad was no more a Communist than a baseball bat. The FBI guy was off base. It was a dumb mistake. Donavan's mistake.

On Sunday, I read the sports page predictions about the coming pennant race. Dodgers. Dodgers. Dodgers. And the Yanks. I didn't care. Then I went through the funny papers. They weren't funny.

Flipping through the rest of the paper, I came across a headline:

NEW SUBVERSIVE BOARD OPENS HEARING ON REDS

The story below it read:

Hearings on whether the Communist Party and its members must register as part of a foreign-controlled agency got under way today after the new Subversive Activities Control Board had ruled it had power to handle the case.

Everywhere I looked, there was Communism. Things were so bad that I did homework to take my mind off it. Then I read some *Black Mask,* looking for detective tips. I needed them.

That night the family listened to our favorite comic radio show, *Jack Benny.* I didn't laugh.

When I went to bed, I couldn't think of the last time Kat and I hadn't talked over a weekend. Dying to tell her about the FBI visit, I wanted to call her. But she'd been awful on Friday, so I didn't.

She didn't call, either.

Earlier in the day, I thought I had figured everything out. But as the hours passed, it seemed unlikely the FBI would come just because Donavan told them to.

There had to be other reasons. But I hadn't a clue.

Monday morning I asked Dad if I could borrow a blue necktie.

"A necktie? That's a rarity. What's happening?"

"Rally for the Dodgers at school. We're supposed to wear blue."

He laughed. "Maybe I should wear something blue too. This has to be our year, right?"

I was in front of our building before eight, tie in place, waiting for Kat as usual. Though it was April, it felt like March. Over my shirt and tie, I wore the newest sweater my grandma had made me.

Now that I was about to see Kat, I felt uneasy. But when she finally came, wearing a blue Dodger sweatshirt,

I had to smile. At the corner, she dropped a letter into the mailbox.

"What did you mail?" I called.

"Box tops for the Secret Code Maker," she said, which made me feel even better.

"Got a lot to tell you," I said.

Before I could say anything, she said, "Wait. Are you wearing anything blue?"

"Tie."

"Did you go to the Saturday movie?"

I shook my head.

"How come? They were showing that detective movie. You love them."

"Didn't want to."

She said, "My aunt was boring." Then she went on about her boring aunt as if she wasn't boring, as if she didn't want me to talk about anything else. It was Friday all over again.

I stopped.

Kat stopped, too. "What is it?"

"Friday."

She frowned, shoved up her glasses, and started to walk again. Fast.

I caught up to her. "It was bad."

She shook her head.

"You forget?" I said. "Donavan called me a Commie. Got everyone to think so. The guys wouldn't let me play punchball. You weren't so great either."

"Sorry," she said, looking all ways except at me. "I didn't know what to do."

"Why do you think Donavan did that?"

"How would I know?" she said, and walked faster.

I grabbed her arm. "Wait a minute. Do you believe him? You think I'm a Commie?"

She shoved my hand away and kept going.

"I'm not!" I yelled at her back. She didn't stop.

For the rest of the way to school I followed ten paces behind her. I felt lower than a splat of spit on the sole of my shoe.

In class, after the Pledge, Donavan said, "We need to make a seat change."

That was unusual. We'd kept the same seats the whole year.

"Pete," said Donavan, "gather your books. I want you to sit over there." He pointed to the last desk in the far row. Where no one sat.

"How come?" I said.

"Because I told you to."

"Is it because—"

"Pete Collison, I've asked you to do something."

"Sir, I'm not—"

"You may go there, or to the principal's office."

I looked toward Kat. She didn't turn around. I sat for a few seconds, wishing I was an ice cube so as not to drip tears. Then I grabbed my books, walked to the back of the room. I dropped into the end desk like an anchor into the ocean.

The kids shifted around, waiting for Donavan to say more. All he said was, "Joel, you're doing Norway."

Joel clomped to the front of the class and began his report. The only words I heard were *"It's not fair."* They repeated in my head like the slapping of a flat tire on the road.

During morning recess, I wedged myself into a corner of the schoolyard, hands deep in pockets. On the wall over my head was a sign that read Shelter. It was the place to go if an atom bomb dropped or your teacher had already blown you to smithereens, like mine had.

I pretended not to watch the punchball game, as if I didn't care. But I did watch. And I did care. And I was getting madder by the minute. *It's not fair. It's not fair.*

Back in class, Donavan announced it was time to go into the assembly hall for the Dodger rally. The class moved toward the door, everyone bumping and jostling to be near the front. I stayed in my seat.

"Move on out, Pete," Donavan called. "You can't stay here alone."

I plodded to the back of the crowd and followed my excited classmates to the assembly hall. They lined up, me last. No one told me. I just knew it was my new world.

Once in the hall, we sat on hard folding chairs. I kept my eyes on the low stage up front. To one side stood a black upright piano, which no one ever played. On the stage were flags: U.S., New York State, New York City, and even a Brooklyn Dodgers flag. They hung there lifeless.

An eighth-grade teacher named Mr. Malakowski—we called him "Mr. Mal"—was in charge of the rally. He was a big guy—kids said he had been an army drill sergeant. His square jaw was always gray, like he needed a shave. He wore double-breasted gray suits with enormous shoulder pads and flashy ties. Today he had on a blue one. Like mine.

"Okay, PS Ten," he began loudly. "This is Brooklyn Dodger day."

The kids cheered.

I did, too, a little.

"We're all here to root for the Dodgers to win the pennant."

More cheers.

"Against the Giants."

Louder cheers.

"Here's our team," said Mr. Mal. One by one, eighth graders ran onto the stage. Each one held a large piece of paper with the name of a Dodger player written on it in blue crayon: Reese. Hodges. Branca, Campanella, Robinson, and so on. Cheers and applause as the kids took center stage.

"And here are the other teams!" cried Mr. Mal.

More eighth graders stepped up holding signs for the National League teams: Chicago, Cincinnati . . . until, finally, Giants. Boos and jeers filled the hall.

Mr. Mal stepped forward: "Remember, kids, this is the year we won't have to say 'Wait till next year.'"

With that, the kid with the Giants sign grinned and tore his paper in half. That brought a *whoop!* The hall went wild.

That was when I had my big idea. I was like the Giants. The one nobody liked. Kat wouldn't talk to me. None of the kids would play ball or sit in the movies with me. My class seat was nowhere. Okay. Fine. If I was going to be treated as an outsider, I'd *be* an outsider. From now on, I'd be a Giants fan.

On the stage Mr. Mal was shouting, "Let's stand up and give one last cheer for the Dodgers."

All the kids stood up and yelled . . . except me.

Pete stayed in his seat, his mouth shut tight. Then he yanked off his blue tie and stuffed it into his pocket.

Pete Collison, the only Giants fan in Brooklyn.

10

The only way they could have made the school day last longer was if they had made the clock run backward. But at three, the dismissal bell finally rang. Kat didn't even pretend to wait for me. I came out of the main doors alone and stood on the top step, watching the other kids messing around with their friends, feeling as empty as a discarded candy wrapper. Loners live alone, I reminded myself as I started for home.

Passing the newspaper booth, I grabbed a *Post* for Ma and glanced at the headlines.

UN GETS PROPOSAL FROM NORTH KOREA
FOR PEACE PARLEY

SYRIA AGREES TO WITHDRAW TROOPS FROM
DISPUTED ISRAEL BORDER AREA

I made up my own.

PETE COLLISON ACCUSED OF BEING A RED
KAT BOYER DUMPS BEST FRIEND
PETE STRIKES BACK BY BECOMING A GIANTS FAN
BROOKLYN FURIOUS
PETE DOESN'T CARE

It was only when I got to the other side of the booth that I saw Kat sitting on the curb. Her tin Nancy Drew lunch box was in her lap; her cowgirl book satchel was by her side. She was eating an apple.

I stopped.

When she saw me, she stood up. "Sorry about this morning," she said. "And school. I didn't know what to say. Stinks that Donavan moved you." She held out the apple. "Want a bite?"

I said, "We still friends?"

She offered a small shrug and a smile to match. "Hope so."

In my whole life, I had never felt like giving any girl a hug. Right then I could have hugged Kat. I did what I could: took a bite of her apple.

We walked toward home without talking. At first, the silence felt good. But I could tell she wanted to say something.

Sure enough, she stopped, looked at me, and said, "Okay, still best friends, but I need to know: If the Commies took over America, would your dad be sitting pretty?"

"You serious?"

"Come on, Pete. Your dad is a Red, right?"

"What makes you think that?"

"My father said so."

That hit me like a beanball. I wasn't sure Kat's father had even met Dad.

"He really said that?"

"Cross my heart, hope to die. Donavan told him and Toby's father that on Parents' Night."

"How come?"

"I don't know."

We started walking again. I said, "My dad teaches American history at New City College."

"So?"

"What's my grade in history?"

"A."

"Right. 'Cause my father is always drilling American history into me. Can you say the Declaration of Independence?"

"Nope."

I said, "'We hold these truths to be self-evident, that all men are created equal, that they are endowed by their Creator with certain unalienable rights, that among these are life, liberty and the pursuit of happiness.'"

"What's your point?"

"My dad says that's the most important sentence ever

written." Then hoping I could put an end to the talk about him, I added, "So my dad knows what America is about."

Kat pushed up her glasses and said, "I hate politics. What are we doing today?"

I said, "I'll slam you at stoopball."

"Yeah, right. I'll kill you."

It was one of the nicest things anyone ever said to me.

When we got to my apartment, we headed for the kitchen. I took the milk bottle from the fridge, shook it to mix in the top cream, and then poured out two glasses. Added two soupspoons of Ovaltine chocolate powder. Got a couple of Twinkies packets.

As we ate, I considered telling Kat about the visit from Ewing and what he had said. But I didn't want to go back to talking Reds.

Kat took a second Twinkie. "Think you'll ever get a TV?"

"Keep asking," I said, glad we were being normal.

On the way out the door, Kat glanced at the family photos on the wall and said, "Your parents are so different."

"What do you mean?" I said, ready to hit back if she gave me more hard time.

"My parents fight a lot."

"About what?"

"I . . . I don't think they like each other."

"Sorry."

"Sometimes," she said softly, "I like your parents better than my parents."

"They're okay," I said, but her saying that made me feel good.

Right down my street was a brownstone house that had a fire hydrant in front of it, so no parked cars. That was where Kat and I always played stoopball. You played stoopball, a kind of baseball, by throwing a rubber ball, a Spaldeen, against the stoop steps. If the other guy caught the ricochet, it was an out. Three outs an inning, nine innings. But if the ball went past the sidewalk and hit the ground once, that was a single; two bounces, a double; three bounces, a triple; over the whole street, a home run.

We played for an hour. I beat her fifty-two to forty-six.

"See?" I said as we headed back to my place. "If I was a Commie, how come I beat you?"

"I never said *you* were a Commie. Said your dad was."

"Okay," I said, "got something gigantic to tell you."

She glanced at me, curious.

"From now on," I said, "I'm rooting for the Giants."

Kat halted like a bumper car hitting the Great Wall of China. "Are you crazy?" she shouted.

"Nope," I said. "Giants fan." I made a fist, kissed my knuckles, and rubbed them over my heart so she knew I meant business.

Kat glared at me. "If you aren't insane," she said, "you are totally nuts. You live in Brooklyn. Dodger territory. The whole class roots for the Dodgers. The whole school. The whole world. Okay, maybe a couple kids go for the Yanks, but that's just them being screwy. Nobody is a Giants fan in Brooklyn. It isn't allowed."

I said, "Leo Durocher went from managing the Dodgers to the Giants."

"Everybody hates him."

"It's a free country."

"Not for Giants fans. I mean it. Why can't you be like everyone else?"

"In school Donavan said I'm different. And everyone is treating me that way. So I'll *be* different. A Giants fan."

"Your family roots for the Dodgers."

"Only my father and my brother. My mother doesn't care."

"The Giants won't even get close to the pennant."

"Oh yeah, come September, the Giants will win and you'll be saying what Dodger fans always say, 'Wait till next year.' How much you want to bet?" I put out my hand. "Five thousand dollars."

She shook it, saying, "Giants—automatic dead last." She cocked her head to one side and said, "You know what? Since you've decided to become a Giants fan, which is, face it, no different than being a Commie, maybe you are a traitor."

We both laughed.

Kat left a little before five. As she headed down the hallway toward the elevator, she called, "Call you tonight for history."

"Sure."

She smiled. "Catch you later, traitor."

I went back to my room. Thinking, *I'm the only Giants fan in Brooklyn,* I ripped down the Dodger posters and pennant.

11

As usual, when dinner began, Ma asked, "How was school?"

Bobby, thumping the bottom of the ketchup bottle as if he was angry at it, began to talk about which speaker they were going to get for his school's June graduation. His principal had chosen the president of the Brooklyn Savings Bank.

"Makes me so mad," he said. "Bunch of pinko students want to get the head of the Brooklyn Longshoremen's Union instead. Bet you anything they were paid to do it by Commies."

I stopped eating and eyed Dad to see his reaction. He

was looking at Ma as if he hadn't heard Bobby, which told me he had heard.

Ma said, "Simply because you disagree with people doesn't mean you have to insult them."

"Reds deserve insults," Bobby replied. "Bunch of traitors. Should be kicked out of the country."

I was sure Bobby had no idea what his words meant to me. As for Dad, he stared at his plate of meat loaf as if he'd been served poison. Bobby's words had upset him.

I waited for more response from him. It took a bit before he looked up and said, "Insults only get you insults," which seemed feeble after his reaction.

Bobby was about to say something else but Ma cut him off by turning to me and saying, "How was your day?"

"Nothing special."

To Dad she said, "And your school, dear?"

Dad talked about a college committee on which he served, some decision they were attempting to make. Except he didn't seem to care. I was sure his mind was still on Bobby's words. *Why?*

Soon as he stopped talking, Ma jumped in, telling us about a problem student she was working with. "His father is fighting in Korea," she said. "He had been in the Pacific during the war."

"That's rough," muttered my father.

Ordinarily, that would have been Dad's cue to start talking history, politics, General MacArthur, and Truman. He stayed mum. I didn't think Dad was a secret Communist, but *something* Bobby had said about reds had bitten him. I tried to think of ways to find out what it was.

Ma started to chitchat: Schedules, plans, who was doing what and when. She soon ran out of things to say and the silence was back, the kind of silence that gets louder every minute. I tried to find a way to get into Dad's thoughts.

Unable to stand it anymore, I finally blurted out, "Dad, if the Commies took over America, would you be sitting pretty?"

Bobby and Ma gawked at me as if I were a Roswell alien.

Ma touched my arm and was about to say something when Bobby said, "Why in the world would you even ask such an idiotic question?"

Keeping my eyes on Dad I said, "Just want to know."

Dad cleared his throat, threw a glance at Ma, and said quietly, "Pete, where in the world does that question come from?"

I said, "Coming home from school, Kat asked me that."

"What a dope," said Bobby.

"She's not."

"Pretty stupid to ask that question."

"Smarter than you!"

"Shh," Ma said, "that's enough."

Dad said, "Pete, what made Kat ask that?"

Already sorry I'd spoken, I sat there, not knowing how to get out of it.

"Pete?" Dad pushed.

I took a breath. "Mr. Donavan said that you were a Commie. Said I was, too. Said it to the whole class."

That sucked the air out of the room. Dad looked at Ma. Ma looked at Dad. They talked that way sometimes, a silent, secret language.

Bobby, leaning in, was gripping the edge of the table with two hands. "Donavan said Dad was a Commie?"

"Yeah."

"Why would he say that?"

"I don't know," I said. "Something about Parents' Night."

To Dad, Ma said, "You were there. Did something happen that night?"

Dad thought for a moment. "I talked to Mr. Donavan about how he teaches history. I told him I didn't think there was enough being taught about the history of Negroes or the working man."

Bobby said, "Why'd you do that?"

"It's what I teach my students," said Dad.

"Not too smart," said Bobby.

"Bobby!" said Ma sharply. To me she said, "Pete, it's wrong of your teacher to say that to anyone."

"I know. Just asking if it's true."

Bobby said, "That's the goopiest question I ever heard."

"What's wrong with asking?" I cried.

Dad, paying no attention to him, said to me, "Let me get this right: Kat was asking if the Soviet Union—China,

North Korea—Communists—took over the United States, would I be 'sitting pretty'?"

I gave the smallest nod ever nodded.

"Pete," said Dad, "I'm *not* a Communist."

"Satisfied?" said Bobby.

All I could think was, *Donavan lied. The FBI lied.* Next second I remembered how strongly Dad reacted to what Bobby said about Commies, so I *wasn't* satisfied. Something was not being said. To Dad I said, "Then . . . what are you?"

"Anti-Communist!" shouted Bobby.

No one paid attention to him. Ma and Dad went back to eye talk.

Dad turned to me. "Was there more to Kat's question than you've said?"

I sat there determined not to talk about the FBI. But I did say, "Donavan told Kat's dad that you were a Commie."

Dad said, "How about you and I have a chat after dinner?"

"Do we have to?"

"You asked the stupid question," said my brother.

"Good Lord, Bobby," said Dad, "there's no such thing as a stupid question."

"He should know the answer," Bobby threw back.

We sat there, no one eating, everybody tense. Wanting to shove the talk in a different way, I said, "And another thing: From now on I'm a Giants fan."

"You're *what?*" screamed Bobby.

"A Giants fan."

"Since when?" asked my father. He looked bewildered.

"Today."

"You know something?" Bobby shouted. "You're a jackass."

"Well, guess what?" I threw back. "Season started today. Philly beat the Dodgers. Giants beat Boston. Guess who's in first place? Giants!"

"You are a total toad!" Bobby yelled back.

I escaped to my room, threw myself on my bed, promised myself I was *not* going to talk about Commies and Reds anymore, grabbed my *Black Mask,* and started to read.

Twenty minutes later, I was still reading when Dad poked his head into the room. "Okay, Pal, we need to talk."

I didn't want to, but I got up from my bed and followed Dad into the radio room. He grabbed the checkerboard, set it on the low table in front of the couches, and laid out the pieces. We always played checkers when we gabbed. Though I had no intention of talking, Dad said, "Go ahead," and we began to play.

After a bit he said, "How come you're rooting for the Giants?"

"Want to."

"That's a major decision."

"Yeah."

"With Bobby and me for the Dodgers, there are going to be some arguments around here."

Sure baseball was not what Dad wanted to talk about, I didn't pay attention to the checkerboard. So he pulled a triple jump and without asking, laid out the pieces again.

I peeked up at him. "You sore about the Giants?"

"Nope."

"Really?"

Dad looked at me. "There's nothing wrong with being different from your family."

"Like Bobby?"

He grimaced. "Yeah, like Bobby."

"All he thinks is about himself."

"Teenagers have been known to do that."

The game went on. As I waited for Dad to say what he had on his mind, the clicking pieces reminded me of a time bomb.

Finally I said, "Were you different from your family when you were Bobby's age?"

Dad had been about to make a move, but his hand hovered over the checkerboard like a stuck helicopter. His breathing deepened. His eyes were on the checkerboard, but it was as if my question had tossed him to another place, a place where I couldn't follow.

He fumbled in his shirt pocket, pulled out a pack of Camels, and knocked the pack on the back of his hand until a cigarette popped up. "Coffin nails," he said, and then added, "Smoking stinks."

I said, "But you do it anyway."

"Black coffee and bad cigarettes kept me alive during the war. They'll probably kill me in the end."

Head bent, Pete's dad drew out a cigarette with his lips. That saved him from using his wounded arm. And from looking at Pete. From another pocket, he took out a dull metal Zippo lighter, the only thing he carried from his war years. He flicked a flame, lit his cigarette, inhaled, snapped the lighter shut. He blew smoke out of his nose, picked a tobacco scrap from his lips, and brushed it away. Then he put the lighter away and, with the back of a thumb, smoothed his mustache. The checkers game forgotten, he stared into his cloud of cigarette smoke as if something or somebody might be there. Pete's question hovered in the air, a ghost nobody wanted to see.

Dad came back to me and said, "That question Kat asked . . . and what your teacher said . . . Communists and all. That get to you?"

"Some," I said, not understanding how his question connected to mine.

"What did you tell Kat?"

"Said . . . you weren't a Communist."

"I'm not."

Remembering what the FBI guy said, I felt uneasy. "Then how come Donavan said that?" I might have asked— but was too scared to—the same thing about the FBI.

"He probably thought my suggestion that he should teach more about the working man and the Negro people makes me a Communist."

"Why?"

"These days, people who work for civil and union rights are often called Communists, and subversive."

"Subversive?"

"Someone who's trying to secretly overthrow the government."

"*That* what you're doing?"

"Of course not. That doesn't mean America can't be improved."

I went back to my original question. "But when you were a kid—*were* you different?"

His face became tense. "Why are you asking that? Different in what way?"

"Well . . . you know . . . like being a Commie . . ."

Pete's dad dragged deeply on his cigarette, and blew out smoke, laying down a thicker smoke screen. Once, twice, he coughed, then mashed the cigarette out in the ashtray. He lit another right away. The lighter snapped shut like a whip.

"Was I ever a Communist?" he said. "The answer is, yes."

Horrified, the best I could do was whisper, "You were? But you said—"

"It was 1934," he said quickly, as if wanting to get it out. "I was nineteen. I went to a Communist Party meeting and signed on."

Shaken, I said, "How . . . come?" I kept my eyes on his face. Far as I could tell, he was staring at the family picture. Then he turned back to me and said, "Clemenceau—he was a French prime minister—said, 'Not to be a socialist at twenty is proof that you have no heart. But to be one at thirty is proof you have no head.'"

"Socialist same as Communist?"

He shook his head. "In a nutshell, Pete, socialism is a

system where the community, the working people, own the businesses and factories, and they share the profits and the wealth made from what they produce. That's the theory, anyway. Communism is the Soviet Union's form of socialism. It's not democratic. In fact, the Soviet Union is a horrible dictatorship. Murdering people who disagree with you isn't my idea of socialism."

"And you were nineteen when you joined?"

His eyes came back to me. "Right."

"You a socialist now?"

"Yup."

"So, you're a . . . socialist . . . anti-Communist?"

"That would fit."

"Then why'd you join the Commies?"

"Back then the Communists talked about how hard things in America were. That was true. They also talked about how great things were in Soviet Russia. That was false, though I didn't know it yet."

I said, "Did anyone know you were a Communist?"

"I never told my family. Of course, your mother knows. Now, you do. No one else."

I thought, *The FBI does.* I wanted to tell him, but Dad was acting so . . . so different, I couldn't get myself to say it. He might even get mad at me for talking to Ewing.

"Pete," he went on, "I grew up during the Great Depression. People called it the hardest of hard times. It started in 1929. Twenty-five percent of the population out of work. That was the official figure. It was probably

74

worse. There were huge problems. The Dust Bowl. Racism. Poverty. Illness. Lots more. The point is, for many, America had failed." He squashed his cigarette into the ashtray, lit another.

"My father was a toolmaker," he went on. "A good one. Not that it mattered. He was out of work for five years, Pete. *Five.*"

That was the first time I *ever* heard Dad talk about his dad.

"What was your dad's name?"

"Tom. Here's a fact about being out of work," Dad went on. "The longer you're out of work . . . the less likely you'll find work. It's the opposite of what you need.

"My father couldn't find work. My mother did. As a waitress. My sisters worked, too. Small jobs, when they could get them. You know, sweeping streets, handing out fliers. Cleaning toilets. Puny pay, but it's like those signs poor people hold up: 'Brother, can you spare a dime?'

"It was my mother who kept us going. It didn't matter if she was sick or felt bad, she worked twelve hours a day."

"Did you work?" I asked.

Dad rubbed his bad arm, as if it was hurting, and stared into his smoke again. "No," he said, as if talking to the smoke.

"Why not?"

"I wanted to be in school."

"That okay with your family?"

He flexed his bad arm, and then said, "My mom, being

a waitress, brought in some money, plus food. Hard times, maybe, but people left food on their plates."

Once again, he didn't answer my question.

"Out of work, my father was going nuts. He was depressed. Angry. Let me tell you something, Pete. It's humiliating to be out of work when you have a family to support. Sometimes my father blamed himself. Or America. Or capitalism. He began to think the Communist system might be better.

"Back then, during the Great Depression, there were lots of news stories coming out of Communist Russia about how great it was there, that jobs were easy to get there. My dad wanted the whole family to go. My mother refused."

"Why?" I said, wanting to make connections between the things he was saying and *not* saying.

"She wouldn't go to a Communist country. And no surprise, my parents' marriage turned bad."

"Was your dad a Communist?"

"Not at all. Just desperate for work. People like to forget, but back then, thousands of Americans, ordinary people, went to Soviet Russia to find work. Sure, some went because they believed in Communism. Most went for a job, to live."

"What happened to them?"

"Things worked for a while until Stalin started putting them in labor camps. Or killed them."

I think my mouth dropped open.

"Here's a story for you. Once, Stalin gave a speech. When he was done, everyone stood up and the applause went on for eleven minutes until some guy finally sat down. That night the guy was arrested. Disappeared."

I said, "*Did* your father go to Russia?"

Dad just sat there.

"Dad . . . what happened to him?"

"I think he died."

"When?"

"In 1935, 1936. Not certain."

"Where?"

Dad stared at his cigarette, and then stubbed it out. The smoke spiraled up, then disappeared, like his answer.

How could he not know what happened to his father?

He remained silent. His silence was like a wound he didn't want me to see. I didn't see the wound but I sure saw the bandage. Which meant I was sure he was not telling me everything.

He lit another cigarette. If cigarettes were coffin nails, he had become a full-time carpenter.

"Anyway," he went on, "with my father thinking the way he did, I told myself that maybe the Soviet Union—and socialism—was the answer. I also believed in unions, civil rights for the Negro people, equality for women. Not that you have to be a socialist to believe in those things. But lots of politicians who were opposed to civil rights, unions, and women were saying the Soviet Union was awful.

"There's an old saying, 'My enemies' enemy is my

friend.' Not necessarily so. In fact, it's bad history. But I came to believe the Soviet Union was a good place, partly because the Communists in America supported many of the things I believed in, and partly because lots of people who stood against the things I believed in were also, like I said, against the Soviet Union."

"Were you right?"

"No. Dead wrong. The Soviet Union was awful. But before I learned that, I joined the Communist Party."

I said, "What was it like being a Communist?"

"I only went to one meeting. It was boring and not what I was looking for. I never went back to another."

"But you signed up."

He nodded. "I was a teenager, Pete. *Nineteen*. Looking for action against those hard times."

"You sorry you joined?"

"Pal, it's a cliché, but in life's journey, if you don't take some wrong turns, you aren't going anywhere."

"You mean, like how you feel about me rooting for the Giants?"

A smile broke through. "You got it."

"Can I tell Kat what you told me?"

He shook his head. "Absolutely not."

"Why not?"

Dad hesitated. "Ever hear of the McCarran Act?"

I shook my head.

"It's the law. President Truman said it was a bad law

and vetoed it but Congress overruled his veto. The Mc-Carran Act does many things, among them, allowing the government to make a list of people they believe are subversives—troublemakers who want to disrupt our government. If there's a national emergency, subversives can be rounded up. Put in prison camps."

"You on the list?" I cried.

"I have no idea. I don't want to be, but it's possible."

"But you only went to one meeting."

He lifted a shoulder. "I'm asking you not to tell anyone—not even Kat—about what I've told you. It's not safe."

"But you're not—"

"No one needs to know. Look, Pete, I'm a historian. I study the past. But these days your past can mean a bad future."

I could almost see Ewing standing there. It made me sick.

"Don't worry," Dad said. "I'm small potatoes. I doubt they're interested in me."

Knowing that the FBI *was* interested, that Dad was in trouble, really scared me. I was also worried that if I told Dad about the FBI, the way Ewing instructed me to, things might get worse. Add in my feeling that Dad wasn't telling me everything—about his father, if he was on that subversive list, why his family didn't want him to go to school—and I didn't know what to do.

Next moment he stood up and said, "I once promised

myself that if I ever had kids I'd never let them down. If they asked, I'd tell them the truth. You and Kat still friends?"

"Think so," I mumbled.

"She's a great kid. Even if you disagree about politics, you can be friends." He moved toward the door. "Okay, Pal, anytime you want more talk, we'll talk. Remember, family get-together on Sunday."

I don't know what my face was saying, but he said, "Families are important, Pete. We don't get together that often."

When he went out of the room, all I could think was, *What is he keeping secret?*

14

I lay on my bed and stared at the ceiling. There was a crack I'd never noticed before. Made me think: You can look at something your whole life and not notice it. Like looking at a dime. Like looking at my dad. Or his dad. Like looking at my whole family.

I told myself it was better not to tell Dad about the FBI visit because it would upset him even more. Except that wasn't the true reason. I didn't tell him because what he said—and didn't say—frightened me. Because another thought had crept in: Maybe Dad, when he was a kid, did something really bad. Maybe that's why he was cagey. Maybe that's why the FBI was after him.

Or was the FBI coming after Dad to learn about his father? Ewing had asked about him. Except, Dad told me his father died.

"Hey, Bobby?" I called over the partition in our room.

"What?"

"You know anything about Dad's dad?"

"Who?"

"Dad's dad. Our grandfather. The one we never saw. The one who died."

Silence, then, "Why you asking?"

"Curious. What happened to him?"

"You're Dad's favorite. Ask him. He tells you his secrets, not me."

"What are you talking about?"

"Well, what was he telling you about before, anyway? His dad?"

"Never mind," I said.

"My point exactly." After a moment, Bobby asked, "You really a Giants fan?"

"Yeah."

"Idiot."

I went back to wondering about Dad and his dad. All of a sudden, a whole new thought crawled into my head: Maybe Dad's dad was still alive.

I heard the phone ring in the kitchen. A minute later Ma poked her head in. "Kat's on the phone."

I leaped off my bed, grabbed my history homework from my desk, and ran down the hall.

"Hey," I said into the phone, "want some help from a first-place Giants fan?"

Kat said, "Wasn't why I was calling." Her voice was tight, her breathing hard, as if she'd been running.

Right off, I knew something was wrong. "What's the matter?"

"I'm not . . . going to school with you in the morning."

"How . . . come?"

"My father says . . . I can't be friends with you anymore."

"What?"

Took her a moment. "You know. Your dad being a Commie."

I kept the phone to my ear, waiting for her to say she was joking. She didn't. She hung up. When she did, a whole part of my life had hung up, too.

Ma came into the kitchen. "Is something the matter with Kat?" she said. "She sounded agitated."

"She's fine."

"Did you have a good talk with Dad?"

"Fine." I started to walk past her. She put a hand on my shoulder. Her worried eyes searched my face. "We don't want you to be upset about these things."

"I'm not," I said, because *upset* was not the half of it.

In my room, I sat at my desk, wishing my life had not become so awful. I stared at my math book, but couldn't open it. After a while, I realized Bobby was standing behind me.

He said, "Want to see something great?"

"No."

"Come on. You got to look at this."

I looked. He was holding some sort of certificate.

"From that National Advisory Committee for Aeronautics," he explained, a big grin on his face. "My acceptance for the science camp. First step to the moon."

"Can't wait till you go," I said.

His smile turned acid. "When are you going to grow up and learn how the world works?"

I said, "Do me a favor: strap yourself to a rocket and light a match."

I jumped up, pushed past him, went into the radio room, and stood before the family picture hanging on the wall. There we were. The whole crowd.

Who was missing? My grandfather. Where was he?

The longer I stared, the more I felt I was playing that game from the Sunday comics, the one called "What Is Wrong with This Picture?"

I woke up the next morning, tired and cross, remembering that Kat wasn't allowed to walk with me anymore. The thought of going to school and dodging Donavan and the kids seemed as much fun as following circus elephants down the street with a shovel.

I forced myself up. In the kitchen, as I sat in front of a bowl of Grape Nuts, Ma, who was putting my bag lunch together, said, "You look tired."

If she had said "dead," I would have agreed.

Dad eyed me while getting coffee. "We didn't talk about your teacher last night," he said. "I think I should go in and speak to him."

"No!" I cried. "You'll only make things worse." I jumped up to get my school stuff together.

"I'm going," Bobby shouted from the hallway.

"Have a happy!" Ma called.

She came into my room with my paper-bag lunch in her hand and questions in her eyes. I took the lunch. Didn't give any answers.

Out on the street, I couldn't help waiting a couple of minutes for Kat. When she didn't show up, I set off. Figuring there would be mostly headlines about Commies, I avoided looking at the newspaper booth as I went past. I had enough headlines in my head. It was when I got to the other side of the booth that I saw Kat standing there.

I stopped, not knowing what to say.

With an almost smile, she said, "You're late."

If you can be happy and angry at the same time, that's the way I was.

She said, "Sorry about last night. My father was right there. He made me say that."

"I don't get it."

"He doesn't want me to have anything to do with reds. I told him you're not one."

"What's he think will happen?"

She scrunched her face. "Something ghastly. When I told my dad what Donavan said about your father, he blew up and said I had to stop being friends with you. Said if I didn't, he'd send me away. And last night he made me call you."

I knew perfectly well that Dad told me not to tell any-one about our conversation, but I trusted Kat more than anyone else. And by meeting me, she was trusting me, too. Besides, the questions in my head were too big. I needed to share them with her.

I said, "Can you keep a secret?"

"You know I can." She made a cross over her heart.

"It's real bad. Better do it again."

She did.

"You know that question you asked about my father: If the Communists took over . . . ?"

"Yeah."

"I asked him."

"What did he say?"

"A lot," I said.

She started walking. "See ya."

I caught up. "Come on, Kat," I cried. "You're the only one in the whole world I can talk to."

She looked at me, brown eyes full of worry. Took her a moment before she said, "Okay. Tell me during morning recess. I won't play punchball."

"You sure?"

"It's dumb that you're a Giants fan, but we're best friends, right? And we already sent for the Secret Code Maker. So we might as well have *some* secrets, right?"

"Whatever you say—" I almost said "sweetheart." Didn't. I had enough troubles.

Class started, as always, with the Pledge of Allegiance.

I pledge allegiance to the Flag of the United States of America and to the Republic for which it stands, one nation, indivisible, with liberty and justice for all.

I changed "one nation, indivisible" to "one nation and I'm invisible." No one heard. When we hit the end, I spoke "all" extra loud. What I really wanted to shout was, "I am not a Commie!"

Hands folded, eyes front, I sat in my corner desk. No one looked or spoke to me all morning. Not even Kat. I might as well have been sitting on the moon with Bobby. When I raised my hand, Donavan ignored me. When there was a math quiz, before the test monitor gave me a paper, he looked to Donavan, as if asking permission. I got all the quiz answers right but only got 89 percent, because Donavan took off points for things like not making a plus sign clear.

Midmorning, we were doing penmanship, when Donavan suddenly shouted, "Drop!"

We often practiced "Duck and cover" drills in case the Russians dropped an atom bomb on us. We scrambled under our desks, wrapped arms and hands around necks and heads, and waited to see if our world was about to end. The first time we did the drill, a couple of kids started to cry.

"All clear," said Donavan.

We crawled back into our seats, and resumed work, knowing the world wasn't ending—probably not before lunch, anyway.

During recess, while the boys played punchball and the girls jumped rope or played hopscotch, Kat and I went to a corner and sat down. We had twenty minutes.

She drew up her legs, wrapped her arms around them, and waited.

I said, "You can't tell anyone."

"Just tell me."

I started by telling her about the FBI visit, what Ewing said about my father being a Commie, and how he wanted to know about my grandfather, whom I knew nothing about.

Kat kept her eyes forward. "Did you tell your parents?"

"No."

"How come?"

"Because—guess what—Ewing is friends with Donavan. At first, I thought Ewing came because Donavan was working to get my father in trouble. I'm not so sure, now. Then I thought the FBI was trying to find out about my grandfather. Only he's dead. So I don't know what they want."

"You should tell your parents. At least your parents listen to you."

At lunch break, I continued my story, telling how my dad *had* been a Communist years ago but didn't like

Communists now. I said, "I'm worried that maybe he did something else back then—something awful."

When Kat didn't say anything, I asked, "If your father did something terrible, would you want to know?"

"Not sure."

I said, "In *The Maltese Falcon* even though Sam Spade loves this lady, when he learns the truth, that she murdered his partner—and he didn't even like him—he turns her in."

"Yikes."

"So what happens if I find out my dad did something awful?"

Kat shook her head.

"This Sunday my whole family is having a get-together. I was thinking I could find out what Dad did back then from them."

"I don't know. Grown-ups hide stuff they don't like talking about."

"Who does that?"

"My parents."

"What are they hiding?"

"Told you: They don't like each other. It's supposed to be a secret but it isn't. My father is always telling my mother she's stupid. She's not."

"Sorry."

"Yeah, well, I'm sorry your dad is a Red."

"That make us equal?"

Don't ask me why, but we started laughing.

At the end of the day, Kat and I walked home from school, not saying much except to agree that we'd meet by the newsstand next morning.

No one else had spoken to me all day. Kat had been my best friend for a long time. Now she was my only friend.

16

On Wednesday, school stayed stinko. When it was over, I went to my job, reading to Mr. Ordson, the blind man. I'd been working for him for about a year. I got the job through one of our neighbors who knew him. Each time I went, I made a dollar.

I usually went on Thursdays, but he'd asked me to come a day early this week. So by three thirty, I was at his apartment building.

It was an old but grand place, with a blue awning that hung over the entrance like the bill on a baseball hat. To get in, you had to use a buzzer system or ask permission from Mario, the doorman. A short, round guy, Mario always wore a long green coat, a peaked cap, gold braided epaulets on his shoulders, and white gloves, as if he was going to a Halloween party pretending to be a general. When he wasn't carrying packages or standing guard at the door, Mario was in the leather lobby chair, studying newspaper racing forms. When Pete came in, Mario grabbed his arm and whispered, "Hey, Pete: Belmont daily double. Win Me a Song in the fifth. Shadow Sister in the sixth. Sure thing." Mario's world seemed to be full of sure things. But the only sure thing Pete ever saw him do was open doors for other people.

There were two flights of stairs, one on either side of the lobby, but I took the creaky elevator to the fourth floor and rang the bell at apartment 4F. In minutes I heard, "Who is it?"

"It's me, Mr. Ordson. Pete."

The door opened. "Good afternoon, Pete."

Mr. Ordson's Seeing Eye dog, a German shepherd named Loki, poked out his wet nose. His other end wagged like a New Year's Eve bandleader's baton.

As for Mr. Ordson, he was tall and thin, with a dome as glossy as an egg, a face that was narrow and high-cheeked, big ears, and clouded white eyes. He always wore a white shirt, red necktie, and a dark suit with a tiny American flag on his lapel. Sometimes the flag was upside down. There were often stains on his tie and crumbs on his jacket. He wore a wedding ring, but Pete never saw a wife or kids, and

93

Ordson never talked much about himself. He was a listener. Pete read the papers, Ordson listened. It was like working for a mask.

Ordson shut the door behind me and turned on the hall light, a single bulb high on the ceiling. Faded pictures of flowers hung on the wall. Sometimes I wondered who looked at them besides me.

I followed Ordson and Loki down the hallway. The dog's toenails clicked on the bare wooden floor like tiny tap dancers. As always, a card table had been set up in a small, dim room off the hallway. Near a reading chair was a wall of thick Braille books. I could barely see, but it was easy to imagine Ordson sitting in darkness, using his skinny fingers to read and make pictures in his head.

Mr. Ordson switched on the ceiling light for me and sat at one side of the table. I sat opposite. On the table was a pile of the *New York Times*. Next to the papers was a glass of milk, plus three Oreo Creme Sandwich cookies on a pink plate.

Loki lay down on the floor, paws stretched out, chin resting between them. He soon nodded off, breathing deeply. Loki was never more than a foot or two away from his master, and I often wondered if he knew Mr. Ordson was blind.

While I ate, Mr. Ordson pressed his hands together and touched his fingertips to his thin lips, as if praying.

"Well, Pete," he'd say, "how are you today?"

"Fine."

"I don't believe that's entirely so."

Surprised, I looked up. His eyes were like white buttons. "How . . . how do you know?"

"You sound distressed."

I said, "Things . . . things aren't great in school."

"I'm sorry to hear that. What has happened?"

"I . . . I'd rather not say," I answered, feeling uncomfortable.

"That's perfectly acceptable. Let's peruse the papers."

I read the major headlines from the top front page.

"Would you be so good as to read me that main story about North Korea," Mr. Ordson asked.

As I read, he listened, head cocked slightly to one side, as usual, not showing emotion. I heard my own voice not always getting the words right, sounding stupid, stuttering as I tried to make sense of what I was reading.

I reached the end of the column. "Most thought-provoking," Mr. Ordson said, and requested another story.

After I read for about an hour, he said, "Would you like more milk? Cookies? They're in the kitchen if you desire some."

"No, thanks."

"Would you care to talk to me now about what is troubling you?"

"No, sir."

He put his hands together. "Then let us continue."

When my reading was done, Loki and Mr. Ordson

walked me to the front door. Mr. Ordson opened it and held out my silver dollar pay. He was the only one I knew who used dollar coins. As I stepped into the hall, he said, "Pete, please know that I am an expert listener."

"Yes, sir," I said.

"As you may have noticed, I have big ears."

The door shut behind me. I heard him snap off the light and walk back down the dark hall. I stood for a bit, thinking that maybe I needed a grown-up to talk to, someone not connected to this business. I even had this thought: *Blind men can't tell if you're invisible.*

I walked home. Got Ma's paper. On the front page was a headline and story:

BEING A RED CALLED "HIDEOUS MISTAKE"

Marc Lawrence, Hollywood actor and specialist in gun-man roles, told the House Committee on Un-American Activities today that he had signed a Communist Party card in 1938. Now, he said, he viewed his action and the associations that followed as a "hideous mistake."

It was like what Dad said. Except this guy was telling his story to a government committee. Would Dad have to do that? It was that moment that I decided I had better tell him about the FBI visit. Besides, if I told him, I might get some answers to my unanswered questions.

I could almost hear Sam Spade saying, "Hey, sweetheart, want to find the truth? Tell the truth."

That's why, when dinner was over, I said to Dad and Ma, "I need to tell you something."

"Don't mind me," said Bobby.

"It's none of your beeswax," I said.

"You know what you are?" said Bobby. "A joke that's not funny."

"Better than being funny without a joke," I threw back.

To me Dad said, "Let's clean up, then talk."

After washing dishes, I went to get those FBI cards so I could show them to my folks. But when I flipped through the *Black Mask,* I found only one. I searched around my desk. Not there. Around my bed. Not there.

Dad stuck his head into my room. "Your ma and I are in the radio room."

Holding the one FBI card as if it was a poison pill, I went down the hall.

Ma and Dad sat next to each other on the couch.

Dad said, "Okay, Pete, what's on your mind?"

I handed Dad the FBI card. He took it, read it, and looked up as if he'd been stung. "Where'd you get this?" He gave the card to Ma. She studied it, then me, eyes wide.

"Last Saturday morning," I said, "when you were shopping, I went to the movies, but I left early. Right after I came home that guy showed up."

"Here? The FBI?"

I nodded.

"Did you speak to him?"

Another nod.

Ma said, "Why didn't you tell us?"

Before I could answer, Dad asked, "What did he say?"

"That . . . that you're a Communist."

Their reaction was like watching a newsreel of an atom bomb blast—all shock and no sound.

At last, Dad said, "How . . . did you respond?"

I tried my best to repeat the conversation. As I talked, Ma and Dad kept exchanging looks. Dad took out his cigarettes and lit one. At one point Ma took Dad's hand.

When I finished, I said, "Did I say anything wrong?"

Dad took a deep breath and said, "You did just fine. They have no right to come in here. Not without a warrant."

We sat there, my parents swapping rapid-fire eye talk. I saw something I had never seen before: They were afraid. Knowing your parents are afraid is like being in the middle of the ocean and discovering your boat has a big hole in the bottom.

For the second time, Ma said, "Pete, why didn't you tell us then?"

"I thought it was Mr. Donavan's doing."

Dad squashed out his barely smoked cigarette in the full ashtray. "Pete, the FBI has already spoken to me."

"They did? When? What about?"

"They . . ." He glanced at Ma. "They wanted to know things. I refused to cooperate. I guess they decided to get to me through you. I'm sorry. But I doubt it has anything to do with your teacher."

"But why did that Ewing guy come after me?"

Dad pulled his second cigarette. "They are using you. Trying to put pressure on me. Fishing for information."

"What information?"

He just sat there.

"He gonna arrest you?" I asked.

"Of course not," said Ma.

Dad looked at his shoes. Ma looked at Dad. I heard what sounded like footsteps in the hall—Bobby. "Dad, how'd the FBI know you'd been a Communist?" I asked.

He looked up fast, like a fish with a hook in his mouth, but didn't answer.

It was Ma who said, "It was probably an informer. Someone who knew your dad had been a Communist and told— the FBI."

I said, "Why would anyone do that?"

Dad took out another cigarette. "Maybe the person thought he was helping the country. Or maybe he was bargaining for something. Or . . . or attempting to harm me."

"Who would want to harm you?"

"No idea."

"If you knew who the informer was, would it help?"

He thought, then said, "I suppose if I knew, I might be able to find out what he said. Try to correct it."

Ma said, "It was probably someone from years ago. Someone who knew your dad when he was a teenager and—"

Dad cut in: "The anti-Communist crowd digs deep for that kind of stuff. Tell me again what this FBI agent said about my father."

"He asked if I knew anything about him. You never really told me what happened . . ."

Dad puffed his cigarette. Another answer went up in smoke. Ma sat there, eyes on Dad, letting him be in charge.

I said, "You going to tell Bobby about this?"

Dad said, "Better keep this to yourself for a while."

Ma jumped in. "Of course we'll tell him. But later, Pete. We need to think some."

Dad said, "Okay, Pete, scoot. You're going to have to let your ma and me talk."

I left the room lugging another load of unanswered questions.

17

Back in my room, I searched for that second FBI card.
When I couldn't find it, I turned on my desk radio;
the Boston Braves had beaten the Giants. The Giants were
no longer in first place.

I flumped on my bed like a wet sandbag. A few seconds
later, Bobby appeared at the foot of my bed. "What were
you guys talking about?"

"What do you care?" I said, but wondered if he was
asking to cover for his eavesdropping. I had to admit, suspicion is catching. People get suspicious about you, you
get suspicious about other people.

Bobby said, "Must be something."

"You think this family is stupid, don't you?"

"Guess what. Couple years, I'm off to college and I'm not coming back. All Dad talks about is history. He's living in the past. Ma just tries to get snotty rich kids to like their parents. You? You're nowhere. I'm the only one who's about the future." He went back to his side of the room.

Pushing aside Bobby's outburst, I went over Ma's and Dad's words: that it was an informer who told the FBI that Dad had been a Communist. That someone wanted to hurt him. But why? Then I remembered Dad saying it might help if he knew who the informer was.

Which meant I now had three investigations: What did Dad do when he was a teenager? What happened to his dad? And who was the informer? It was like a real-life detective story. In mystery stories, the private eye starts by looking for the answer to one question. Then he learns he needs answers to lots of questions. Doesn't matter how many. In the end, he learns that all the questions are connected. When he answers all of them, the truth spills like Niagara Falls.

If I were going to start with one question, I'd start with what Dad did. Seemed the easiest. Because if anybody knew something about Dad back then, Grandma Sally would. All of a sudden, I was actually looking forward to the family get-together Sunday.

Thursday morning, I was so tired Ma had to wake me. Feeling like an old sock, I got up and out and met Kat by the newsstand. Right off, I said, "I did what you said. Told my folks about the FBI."

"What did they say?"

"It's a long story. Tell you during recess."

She said, "I have bad news. My father called Mary Geary's father. He fixed it so Mary watches me and tells him if you and I talk."

"An informer."

"I suppose. I don't care. We'll have to meet here after school to talk."

We headed off, talking baseball. With the Giants losing, Kat teased me. I didn't mind. At least she was talking to me. But a couple of blocks from school, she halted. She gave a little wave. "See you at the newsstand," she said, and went off. I walked the rest of the way alone.

In the schoolyard, while kids waited to get inside, no one talked to me. I saw Mary Geary watching Kat. Kat pretended I wasn't there.

Class began regular enough, with me in my corner desk, which was like that island in the middle of the Pacific, Bikini, where they exploded the A-bomb. I guess I was radioactive, too.

Benny Greene, the class clown, was that day's ink monitor. A runt of a guy, he had a buzz haircut, chubby little hands, and a smart mouth. He went round the room, carefully filling the little glass cups set into each desk. Gradually, he worked back to my desk. As he leaned over, his hand jerked. Black ink poured over me.

"Hey!" I leaped up.

"Accident!" cried Benny. He turned toward Donavan.

"Sorry, Mr. Donavan, sir. I know. I should have used red ink." Kids laughed.

Furious, I stood by my desk looking down at my ink-splotched shirt.

Class titters faded when Donavan stood there, not saying anything. "Benny," he said, "I think you need to apologize to Pete."

"Sorry," muttered Benny but slipped in a smarmy smirk.

That tipped me over. I punched his chest as hard as I could. He staggered back. The ink bottle slipped from his hands, hit the ground, and burst. Black ink spattered everywhere. Kids leaped from their desks.

"Pete!" roared Donavan. "That's enough."

Struggling for breath, I shouted, "He did it on purpose! And you wanted him to."

All Donavan said was, "Ben, take your seat. Philip, run to the basement and tell the custodian we had an ink bottle break."

Philip tore out of the room.

I glared at Donavan. If he had gotten closer, I would have punched him, too. He must have guessed, because he didn't budge.

"Pete," he said, "Ben has apologized for his clumsiness. Now let's move on. Take your seat."

"I'm soaking wet!" I shouted, and headed for the door.

"Where are you going?"

"Home to change my clothes. You don't want me here anyway."

Donavan's cheeks turned red, but he didn't say otherwise.

I yanked the door open and looked back. The whole class was staring at me. "And I'm a Giants fan!" I cried, slamming the door behind me.

I galloped home. Soon as I got into our apartment hallway, I stripped off my shirt and headed for the bathroom. Next moment I heard a *thunk* coming from Dad's office.

I froze. "Who's there?"

Bobby stepped into the hall.

I said, "What are you doing home?"

"Had to get something. What's with you?"

"Got ink all over my shirt." I held it up.

"How'd that happen?"

"Accident. What were you doing in Dad's office?"

"Told you. Needed something."

"What?"

"That's for me to know and you to find out," he said.

Fuming, I went to the bathroom, turned on the tub tap, and flung in my shirt. Ink seeped away like blue-black blood.

"See you later," I heard Bobby shout. The front door slammed. He wanted to get away fast.

I washed my chest and dried myself. Leaving the shirt to soak in the tub, I went to my room, where I put on clean clothes. Satisfied, I headed for the front door, only to stop before I got there. What had Bobby been doing in Dad's office?

I went back and looked in.

Think, I told myself. *Think like Sam Spade.* Okay. Any clues? One: that sound: *Thunk.*

Standing in the doorway, I studied the office. As usual, it was so messy it was impossible to tell much. Then I noticed that one of the file cabinet drawers was slightly open.

I ran to the front door, locked and chained it, returned to the office, and yanked out that drawer and shoved it closed. *Thunk.* The same sound I'd heard before. It bounced out a bit, too, the way I found it. Okay: Bobby had opened and shut that drawer. What had he been looking for?

I pulled the drawer fully open and began to flip through the tabs. "Medical." "Books." "Insurance." Ordinary things. But one tab was sticking up slightly, as if it had been pulled but not shoved completely back down.

It was labeled "Frank."

Having no idea who "Frank" was, I lifted the folder out and spread it wide.

Inside were two photographs, one big, one small. The smaller picture was that one I'd seen in Dad's desk: Grandma Sally, a man, my dad's sisters, Dad, and a boy who might have been a friend. I had thought the man was my dad's Uncle Chris. Now I decided the image was sort of like him though not exactly. With all that talk about Dad's dad, it crossed my mind that this might be him.

The larger of the two photographs was a washed-out picture of a man and two boys. Dressed in old-fashioned overalls, the man sort of looked like my dad. Bald. Not too tall. Was *he* Dad's dad?

The older kid was about my age, twelve. The second boy was younger, shorter. The older one of the pair had his arm round the younger boy's shoulder. The kids were grinning, looking like best friends.

I flipped the picture over. In faded black ink—not my dad's handwriting—someone had written "Frank." There was a second name, "Nelson Kasper," written in pencil—Dad's writing. Under that was scrawled "Blaine" and a number, "2573."

Two people, three names, and a number. Which name belonged to whom? Who were they? What did that number mean?

I put the photos back in the folder, replaced the folder the way I'd found it, closed the drawer, and went to my room.

I lay on my bed and began asking myself questions. Had Bobby been looking at those pictures? If so, why? Did he know who Frank, Blaine, and Nelson Kasper were?

Before I knew it, I had fallen asleep. After what seemed like only the next moment, I woke suddenly and checked the clock. It was one o'clock in the afternoon. I had missed almost the whole school day.

My first reaction was to be upset, but then I was glad I didn't have to deal with Donavan and the kids, at least for a while. Instead, I ate lunch, read some, and waited till three. Then I grabbed a couple of Twinkies and headed for the newspaper stand, where I sat on the curb and waited for Kat. When she showed up, I held out a Twinkie.

She took it and sat down by my side. "Benny's a jerk," she said.

"Did Donavan say anything after I left?" I asked.

"Said we should keep away from you. That you were trouble."

"He's the jerk."

"Said you'd be suspended for fighting and leaving school."

"*Suspended?* You're kidding."

She shook her head. "For a day. Tomorrow."

"What about Benny?"

"Donavan didn't say."

"When I got home, my brother was there."

"You tell him what happened?"

"Not really. Thing is, he was supposed to be in school, only he was in my dad's office, looking for something in a file cabinet. I checked. It was some old photos."

"Photos of what?"

"They might be my grandfather and my father when he was a kid. His sisters and some friend, too. On the back side, there were names I never heard of. Oh, yeah, and last night I think Bobby was listening when I was talking to my parents about the FBI."

"When you told them about the FBI, what did they say?"

"They were frightened. And I'm sure Dad's hiding

something. Other thing: My parents think all this is happening because someone—the informer—is trying to get at my dad."

Clutching her lunch box and satchel, she stood up. "Gotta go," she said.

"You know what?" I said, looking up at her. "I really want to find out who the informer is. And find out if Dad did anything, you know, bad."

"You really going to do that?"

"Yeah."

"See you later, traitor," she said with a grin, and started to walk off, swinging her lunch box at her side. Then she stopped and threw me one last question over her shoulder. "What'll happen when you find out those things?" she asked.

I hadn't thought of that.

18

I was in my room late that afternoon, reading a story in *Black Mask*, something called "Take It and Like It," when Ma came home and walked straight into my room.

"Pete," she said, "I received a call at work from your school principal's office. You've been suspended from school tomorrow for fighting and leaving school. What in the world happened?"

"I punched a kid."

"My goodness, Pete. Why?"

"He spilled ink on me. On purpose. Then I came home to change my shirt and . . . I fell asleep."

"Fell asleep?"

"Honest."

"We'll talk about this later. I'm not happy, Pete."

"Think I am?" I shouted as she went down the hall.

At dinner, Ma silently served up the lamb chops and mashed potatoes along with spring peas. When she sat down, she said, "All right, Pete, what happened at school?"

"Ink on his shirt," said Bobby. "Big whooping deal."

"Your brother was suspended from school," said Dad.

"You kidding?" said Bobby. "Why?"

"Fighting."

"What did you do, squirt, beat up some first grader?"

"Shh," Ma scolded. "Pete, you need to tell us what happened."

I just sat there.

"Pete," said Dad, "this is serious. We need to hear."

Grudgingly, I told them everything about what had been going on with Donavan, what he said in class that day, the Commie business, making me read the definitions, and how the kids were treating me. How Kat's father said she and I couldn't be friends. I explained that Benny spilled ink on me on purpose. I said what he said and how I punched him.

Ma's face kept changing, shifting from worry to surprise to anger. Dad just stared at me, his face pale, eyes sad, but mostly tired. From time to time, he swiped a hand across his mouth and mustache, as if to keep himself from talking. Bobby gazed at me with his usual know-it-all look.

Sure enough, when I was done, he said, "First of all your teacher is a mug. Second, the kid who spilled the ink should have been kicked out, not you."

That took me by surprise. Bobby didn't defend me very often.

Ma said, "I don't have much good to say about your teacher."

And Dad said, "I don't think Mr. Donavan is acting the way a teacher should. I need to talk to him."

In a flash, I could see Dad going in, arguing with Donavan. Donavan going right to the FBI . . . "Don't!" I cried. "I can handle it."

Dad sighed. "Are you sure?"

"Yes."

Ma said, "Maybe you should transfer to my school."

"No!" I said even louder, thinking about Kat, my only friend. "I want to stay."

Dad shook his head. "I really need to go in and talk—"

"I don't want you to! You'll make things worse."

No one spoke for a few moments.

"Well," said Ma, "the suspension is only for one day. Let's see what happens." Then she said, "Pete, I don't approve of your punching that boy. But I think you were provoked. And that shirt is ruined. Promise us that if Mr. Donavan continues to treat you unfairly, you'll tell us."

"Fine," I said, but made up my mind not to tell them any more. The thought of Dad going to Donavan with the FBI still sniffing around was too upsetting.

Before I went to sleep that night, I listened to the radio. After winning the opening game of the season, the Giants kept losing. They even lost their home opener to the Dodgers. The Giants were in last place. Like me.

As I lay there, Bobby called from the other side of our partition, "Hey, Pete."

"What?"

"It stinks the way you were treated in school. You're doing the right thing."

"What's that?"

"Not making a fuss about it. It'd only make things worse."

"For who?"

"The family."

"What do you care?" I said. "You said you're the only one who cares about the future."

When he didn't say anything, I got off my bed and I stood by the partition. He was at his desk, a textbook in his hand. He looked up at me.

I said, "What were you doing in Dad's office?"

My question must have taken him by surprise, because he just stared at me. Then he said, "What are you talking about?"

"When I came home, you were in his office."

He turned back to his book. "Getting paper," he muttered.

"You didn't have paper in your hand."

"Couldn't find it."

"It's always on his typewriter stand."

He stared at his book.

I said, "You were going through his file cabinet, weren't you?"

No response.

I pushed. "What were you looking for?"

"Buzz off," he said, and shifted so his back was toward me.

I got into bed still thinking about Bobby in Dad's office. Then Bobby walked out of the room. I got up again and followed him partway to the kitchen, where I heard him pick up the phone. I tried to hear what he said but I couldn't. When he hung up, I scurried back to bed. As he passed through the room, I asked, "Who were you calling?"

He said, "One of my friends you don't know."

"Some stupid girlfriend?"

"If I had a girlfriend she wouldn't be stupid like yours is."

Certain he was up to something, I put him on my list of puzzles. Then I grabbed my *Black Mask* and read the last story: "Death of a Witness." At least Detective Roscoe Carter would solve everything before I turned out the lights.

On Friday, I woke up at my regular seven o'clock only to remember I wasn't going to school. I stayed in bed and heard Bobby move around but shut my eyes and pretended to be asleep as he passed through the room so I wouldn't have to talk to him. I heard Ma going to the kitchen. Dad walking up the hall. Bobby leaving. "Enjoy school," Ma called to him. The door slammed.

Dad stopped in my doorway. "Pete?" he whispered.

When I still faked sleeping, he retreated. The front door clicked. A little later Ma left, too.

There he was, private eye Pete Collison, alone in bed. From somewhere down on the street a car horn dented the stillness. His window rattled slightly. His bed frame creaked. He slept and dreamed he was walking down a long alley, which led to another long alley and then another. When he woke up, he looked around. He hadn't budged. A beam of sunlight had slipped through his window and was pointing to the floor as if accusing it of something. It didn't say what.

I went into the kitchen where my cereal bowl sat on the table, along with spoon, paper napkin, and a box of Grape Nuts. Ma's paper from yesterday was also there. On the bowl was a note.

Call me when you get up xxx Mom

Looking for the sports section in the paper, I came upon a story:

Senator Joseph R. McCarthy of Wisconsin described Secretary of State Acheson today as an "extremely clever" witness. Mr. McCarthy, one of the secretary's sharpest critics, added that Mr. Acheson is "awfully bad for America and awfully good for Communism at home and abroad."

It felt strange reading that. Sure, there had been plenty of talk and newspaper stories about Communism before. Now, all of a sudden, I was connected to it. It didn't matter that I didn't want to be a part of the story. I was.

I ate breakfast. Read the sports. The Giants had lost six in a row. Disgusted, I pushed the paper away and tried to imagine what was going on in school. Maybe history. Or math. I wondered if Donavan had said anything about me.

Back in my room, I grabbed my *Black Mask*, only to realize I'd read all the stories. With nothing better to do, I decided to go to Ritman's and get something new, something with stories about the FBI. That made me remember the missing FBI card.

Certain I'd put the card in *Black Mask*, I went through it one more time, page by page. The card wasn't there.

I searched under my desk and my bed again. Nothing. I opened the little drawer in my desk. Pencils. Erasers. A few baseball cards. Nothing else. I glanced toward the partition and Bobby's side of the room. If Bobby could snoop around Dad's office, I could do the same to Bobby.

I went to his side. He had the same bed and desk as I did. No baseball posters on his wall, just pictures of rockets and jet planes. His acceptance certificate for that summer camp was on the wall, too.

Bobby's desktop was clean and neat, with only a pile of *Popular Science* magazines. It took one glance to see the FBI card wasn't there. I pulled his desk drawer open. Some pencils, a pencil sharpener, protractor, and a slide rule. Under the slide rule was the FBI card.

Questions tumbled in my head like a clown in the circus. Why did he have it? How did he even know I had the cards? Was it from listening in when I talked to Ma and Dad? Had he looked for them? What did he want with it, anyway?

Intending to challenge him directly that afternoon after school, I left the card there so he couldn't deny he had it.

By the time Pete got dressed, it was almost ten. He took two bits from his money can, told himself to stop thinking about Bobby, and headed out. He checked the sky and the street. The sun was bright. The people looked less so. A biplane trailing a Coca-Cola streamer buzzed above like a summer fly.

Pete walked into Ritman's Books and found Ritman behind the counter, smoking and reading a new Adventures into the Unknown. *Ritman looked up, blew a slip of smoke from his nose like a burned-out dragon, and said, "No school, kid?"*

"Had a stomachache. My mother said I could stay home."

"Reading is good for bellyaches." Ritman pointed with his chin. "You know where they are."

"Thanks."

I stepped into the back room, and poked around until I found an *Ellery Queen's Mystery Magazine.* Its cover showed a dead lady mostly concealed by a white sheet. It had a true FBI story, called "Tapped Out." It was about how, during the war, an FBI agent caught a Nazi spy by fixing a tap on the telephone junction box in an apartment basement and listening to conversations day after day.

I read the story and was about to leave the store when I glanced at the supermarket across the street. Bobby and Uncle Chris were coming out the doors.

How come Bobby wasn't in school? Why was he with Dad's uncle? I backed into Ritman's, turned on my detective brain, and watched.

Uncle Chris was a plumber with his own business somewhere in Brooklyn, out near Coney Island. He was an old guy, maybe seventy-five, barrel-chested, with muscled arms and a big mouth to match. He was the kind of guy who kept a fence all around him. If anyone got near, he'd slap you away with sarcastic remarks, or with his fists if words didn't finish the job. He had as much sparkle as a wad of old chewing gum. Pete didn't like him.

I hoped Bobby wasn't telling Uncle Chris about my suspension. Chris would scatter it around the whole family.

The two of them talked awhile, then went different ways.

Behind me, Ritman called, "Hey, Pete, what you staring at?"

I wished I knew.

I got home, my mind full of suspicions about Bobby. My detective mind tried to figure it out but it seemed as if I were walking down endless alleys. I was so lost in my thoughts that when the doorbell rang, I jumped. Right away, I thought of the FBI.

I ran to my parents' bedroom, lifted a Venetian-blind slat, and peeked out. Sure enough, parked across the street was a small black Ford with New York license plate PED459. The FBI had come back.

The doorbell kept ringing.

19

I snuck back down the hallway, stood on my toes, and put my eye to the peephole. Ewing, hat in hand, was standing in the hall. I jumped back. Why was he here?

The bell kept ringing.

Fists clenched, breathing hard, I stood still.

"Pete," called Ewing. "I know you're home. I really need to speak to you."

I didn't move. Just hoped he would go away. After a long silence, I put my eye to the peephole again. He was gone.

I tore back to my parents' bedroom and looked down in time to see Ewing walking across the street toward his car. He got in. The car pulled away.

I took a deep breath, went to my room, and sat on the

edge of my bed, and tried to calm down. I was as wobbly as a three-wheeled roller skate.

Why did Ewing need to speak to me? How did he know I was home?

I went into Bobby's side of the room and pulled out Ewing's card. Bobby said Dad told me all his secrets. Maybe Bobby used the FBI card to call Ewing last night, told Ewing that I knew Dad's secrets and that I'd be home today. That would explain why Ewing came.

Except that would make Bobby an informer. Why would he do that? *He couldn't. He wouldn't.* My thoughts a jumble, I put the card back and started pacing around the apartment.

The phone rang. I wasn't sure I should answer.

When it kept ringing, I decided that if it was Ewing, I'd catch him by surprise and ask him how he knew I was home.

I picked up.

"Hello, love." It was my mother. "Goodness, where were you? You never called."

My mind still churning about Bobby and Ewing, all I said was "Sorry."

"What have you been doing?"

"Nothing. Reading."

"That's good. Have any other plans?"

"No. Did Bobby have school today?"

"Of course. Why? Feeling lonely?"

"No."

"I'll try to get home early."

"Okay."

"You don't sound too great."

"I'm fine."

"Call me if you need anything. Or want to talk."

"Okay."

"Pete, love, you didn't do anything very wrong. You shouldn't have been suspended."

"I know."

I hung up and sat in the kitchen. Looked in the fridge. There was nothing I wanted to eat. I wandered down to my room. It felt empty. I did too. I decided to go back to Ritman's.

Out on the street, I checked for Ewing's car. I didn't see it. Walking, I looked to see if anyone was following me. No one was. When I got to the bookstore, Ritman was still in his place behind his counter, reading. The only thing different was that he had moved on to the newest *Vault of Horror* comic.

"Stomach still hurting?" he said, without looking up.

"Mind if I hang around and read?" I said.

"Reading beats hanging around," he said, without lifting his eyes from the comic.

I went into the back room, found the *Ellery Queen's Mystery Magazine* I had been reading, and went over that FBI story again. It occurred to me that the mysteries in my hands were a lot bloodier than the ones in my head, but the ones in my head were more complicated.

An hour later, I bought the magazine and went to the Rexall Drugstore down the block. Taking an end stool at the food counter, I had a hot dog and a Pepsi for lunch while reading my new magazine. Near two thirty, I made my way to the newsstand. It was too early to meet Kat, so I sat on the curb and read another story, called "A Simple Matter of Deduction."

Simple. I wished.

"Hello, traitor." Kat sat down next to me. "Giants, third place."

I said, "Dodgers, fifth. What happened in school?"

"Not much."

"Donavan say anything about me?"

She shook her head. "What did you do all day?"

"The FBI guy came back." And I told her my suspicions about Bobby.

After that, she stood up. "Gotta get home. My father started checking with my mother about what time I get there. He's worried that I'm hanging out with you."

"You are. How're your parents?"

"Still fighting."

"About what?"

"Their marriage."

We started to walk. She said, "You going to the movies tomorrow?"

"Don't want to."

"Me neither."

"I know," I said, "let's tell our parents we're going to

the show, only we'll meet in that library on Monroe Street. No one will see us there. It opens at nine, same as when the movie starts."

"I'll be there."

"You're an angel."

"Why you saying that?"

"It's what Sam Spade calls his secretary."

"I'm not an angel," she said as she walked off. "Not your secretary, either," she called over her shoulder.

That got us laughing. "See you," I called.

A few minutes later, Mary Geary went by across the street. She was spying on Kat. The whole world was full of spies.

I bought Ma's paper and went home.

Soon as I walked into my side of the room, Bobby called from his side.

"Pete?"

"Yeah."

"Where you been?"

"Walking around. How was school?"

"No classes. The teachers had meetings. So I met with my Rocket Club."

"All day?"

"Mostly."

I put my *Ellery Queen's Mystery Magazine* on my desk next to the *Black Mask*, which I shoved to one side. When I did, the FBI card poked out. Bobby must have put it back in *Black Mask*, hoping I hadn't noticed it was gone.

I called. "You been reading my *Black Mask* magazine?"

"I don't read garbage."

Wishing I could dust for fingerprints, my best deduction was that he'd used the card to tell the FBI I was home.

For the rest of the afternoon I stayed away from Bobby. I read my new magazine, and then listened to the radio. Russ Hodges announced the end of the Giants game, which they lost.

Truth is, I could hardly think about baseball. Mostly I thought about Bobby.

He'd listened to my conversations with Dad. He had been going through Dad's files and looked at those pictures. He had taken that FBI card. Put it back to cover up. He was after something. Was it for himself or the FBI?

What would I do if Bobby was the informer?

Saturday morning I told my folks I was going to the kids' movies. Instead, I walked into the library fifteen minutes after it opened.

The library was a gloomy place, with high ceilings and dull lighting. Cracked brown linoleum covered the floors. Heavy tables, chairs, and bookcases were all dark wood. On the tables were reading lamps with green glass shades that looked like large green mushrooms. Paintings of old-fashioned-looking men with whiskers like Brillo hung on purple walls. The few adults sitting there were reading, though one guy was already asleep. The place had as much life as a funeral parlor.

I didn't go to the library much because kids my age weren't allowed anywhere except a small children's section. That was in a corner, walled in on four sides by low bookcases. The library had a mysteries section, but I'd been told by an old librarian that I couldn't borrow those books till I got to high school.

I went to the children's section and looked for Kat. She wasn't there, so I grabbed a Hardy Boys mystery, *The Secret of the Lost Tunnel,* from the "Boys' Books" shelves. Nothing to go ape about, but it was a detective story.

I was up to Chapter Three when Kat sat down in the chair next to mine.

"Giants in sixth place," she said. "What you reading?"

I showed her the title.

"Are we lost in a tunnel?"

"Worse," I said. "That FBI card came back."

"How'd that happen?"

"Bobby put it back in one of my magazines."

"You sure?"

"Like Ivory Soap: Ninety-nine point forty-four percent sure."

"Find out any more about your dad?"

"No. I'll talk to Grandma Sally tomorrow. Funny: I never spent much time thinking about Dad before. He never talks about himself, except being in the war. Now, I feel I don't know him."

"You're not supposed to learn too much about your parents."

"Is that a rule?"

She nodded. "Parents' rules."

"I'm sorry, children," a voice broke in. It was a young librarian. "I have to ask you to keep your voices down. Someone has complained."

I looked over my shoulder. Across the room, a lady with bright red hair glared at us.

Kat looked too. "Oh-oh."

"What?"

"That lady plays bridge with my mother."

Over the next couple of hours, Kat and I whispered about our usual ten billion things. The biggest was that afternoon's Dodgers—Giants game.

At quarter to twelve, we got up. I checked out the Hardy Boys book. The same librarian who had spoken to us stamped a red ink date on the "Date Due" slip inside the pocket on the back cover. "I'm sorry about that lady." She smiled. "I hope you come again. You have two weeks to get out of the tunnel."

As we walked out, I said, "That librarian was faking being nice."

"No, she's nice."

"What makes you so sure?"

"If you fake a smile, your eyes don't crinkle. Her eyes crinkled."

"How come you know so much?"

She squiggled up her glasses. "I'm tall."

"Monday," I said. "Same time. Same station. I'll tell you what my grandmother says."

"Catch you later, traitor," said Kat, and she ran off.

That afternoon I listened to the Giants and Dodgers game. The Giants lost. Again. It was bad enough that the Giants were losing so often. Listening to the game, I had to admit their announcer, Russ Hodges, wasn't as good as the Dodgers' announcer, Red Barber. They say you win some, lose some. I just wanted to win once. So I put all my thoughts to talking to Grandma Sally tomorrow, knowing she'd be able to tell me Dad's secret.

I couldn't wait.

Ma's family lived in Indiana. I rarely saw them, though she called her mother every Saturday, when long-distance rates were low.

Dad's family lived in New York City, where he grew up. We would get together two, three times a year. I wasn't sure why it wasn't more. I knew my aunts saw each other often. Sister stuff, I guessed.

When we went, Ma and my aunts stayed mostly in the kitchen, cooking and talking about kids. The men sat around in big chairs, like a movie that didn't move, just talked. My cousins and I, from two years old up to fourteen, did what we wanted: played kick the can, stickball, talked baseball, played board games. That part was okay.

This Sunday's get-together was a birthday party for Aunt Louise. It was at Aunt Betty's apartment on Eastern Parkway, out in Brooklyn. By the time we arrived, everybody else was already there. Sometimes I thought my folks got to these gatherings late on purpose to shorten the visit. I hadn't thought much about it before, but now I wondered why.

Aunt Betty's apartment was a musty, cluttered place, like a museum exhibit that never changed. Heavy armchairs covered with yellowish doilies and fringed cloths stood around like stuffed animals. On every table were vases with cloth flowers. Mirrors and faded pictures were on the wall. On the floor were small oval rugs that looked like old scabs. No books. Just magazines and a cabinet radio that was never open.

I only knew a few things about my relatives. I knew Dad's sister, Aunt Betty, made great lasagna. Her husband, Uncle Harry, worked in a hardware store. Dad's other sister, Aunt Louise, did something about real estate. Her husband, Uncle Mort, smoked a pipe and had an insurance business. Uncle Chris—Grandma Sally's brother-in-law—was a plumber. And Dad had just told me that Grandma Sally, his mom, used to be a waitress. That was as much as I knew.

Okay. Dad taught us history, but not much about his family history. How come? That was the first question.

When we got there, Dad and Ma went to Grandma

and talked to her, but not for long. They never did. Second question: Why not?

Then Ma went into the kitchen with the chocolate pudding pie she'd made, and Dad went and sat with the men. Same time, Bobby went over to Uncle Chris. I guess they had become friends.

Third question: When did they become friends and why?

I joined the men, who were talking business and politics. Uncle Mort was a Democrat. Uncle Harry was a Republican. When they argued politics, they flung wads of words at each other like a kids' food fight. Names like Truman, Eisenhower, McCarthy, and Roosevelt were tossed around like bread balls.

Mostly, Dad kept his mouth shut. Now and again, the men would ask him something about history. He'd offer facts, which didn't seem to matter to them. Uncle Chris was mostly quiet, too. He just sat there, frowning and looking cross. Every once in a while, he'd make some sarcastic, angry remark.

Fourth question: Why was Uncle Chris so angry?

Score: Questions 4. Answers 0.

There was a family rule that every kid was supposed to say hello to Grandma. Wanting to talk to her alone, I held back and studied her.

Pete's Grandma Sally was a small, wiry woman with curly, snow-white hair and fierce, iron-gray eyes below black eyebrows. Her face was almost chalk white, with net-like wrinkle lines and a mouth as tight as a vise.

Unlike her daughters, she never wore shirtwaists or high heels, but preferred a formless dress. Today's was pale blue. On her feet were shaggy pink slippers. She took those slippers in a wrinkled paper bag everywhere she went. It looked like the same bag, save that it had a few more wrinkles every time Pete saw it.

At family gatherings, Grandma Sally went straight for a corner chair, where she sat knitting the scratchy sweaters for her grandchildren that were sure to show up at the next family gathering. Her small, bony fingers never stopped working those needles. But even as she knitted, her gaze darted about over members of the family, like the gaze of an old, skinny white cat, choosing where to pounce.

I sat down next to her. "Hi, Grandma."

"Hello, Pete," she said, her needles not stopping. She leaned over slightly so I could poke a kiss on her dry, wrinkled cheek. It was like kissing tissue paper.

"How's school?" she said in her clipped voice.

"Okay."

"You getting good grades?"

"Yes."

"I made your favorite cookies. Cinnamon."

"Thanks."

I'd done my duty and was free to walk away. But this was my chance, and I took it. "Grandma, can I ask you something?"

Needles still clicking, she said, "Depends what it is."

I said, "What was my father like as a teenager?"

The needles halted. She turned toward me. "Which part of your father's life would you like to know about? When he was your age?"

Fighting my discomfort, I said, "No, older. When his— when your husband died."

Her cheeks went white on white. Her jaw clenched. "Why are you asking?"

"Just . . . the other day, Dad was telling me about him."

"What did he say?"

"How . . . how he died."

"He didn't die," she said. "He vanished."

"What do you mean, *vanished*?"

She sat still for a moment then pointed down. "You ever wonder why I wear slippers?"

"Not really."

"The old days, what they called the Great Depression, were bad times. I was a waitress. On my feet all day and night. Just thinking about it, my feet get sore. These slippers make them feel good. They tell me that those days are gone."

I didn't understand why she was telling me that.

"I worked," she continued, her voice as raspy as an old saw, "so I could keep the family together. Because Tom, my husband, couldn't find work. Too proud to take anything except machine work.

"Then one day, he was gone. I never heard from him

again. Not one word. After seven years I had to go to court to get a divorce."

"You have any idea where he went?"

All she said was, "The children were very angry. They told friends their father died. Kids want fathers to be there. He wasn't. I was."

That idea I had before, that my grandfather might still be alive, popped back into my head.

Grandma picked up her needles.

I said, "Did my father . . . do anything when your husband went away?"

The knitting stopped again. She took her time before saying, "After Tom left, your father . . . ran away from home."

"Ran away?" I cried. "For how long?"

"Six years. Left when he was eighteen. I didn't see him again till he was twenty-four."

"But . . . where'd he go?"

"He never told me. He didn't come back until just before going overseas with the army." Her thin lips quivered. "By then, he'd married your mother. Had you kids. Can you imagine? I don't see him for six years and then it's, 'Hello. Here's my wife and kids. Good-bye. I'm off, maybe to be killed.'"

She turned so that she was looking right at Dad. Glaring, really. Next moment she turned livid eyes on me. "Do you know what memories are?" she said. "Dead-end streets. You can't go anywhere with them even if you want to. Not worth trying."

She snatched up her knitting, and the needles began clicking faster than ever. "Go find some of my cookies," she said.

I walked away asking myself why, if my grandfather didn't die, Dad would say he did. And where'd Dad go? Did he really run away from home? To do what? Were those the things the FBI wanted to know, too?

Questions 9. Answers 0.

My cousin Ralph grabbed my arm. "We're going out to play stickball. Come on."

"Later," I said.

I wandered around Aunt Betty's apartment. On her lace-covered bedroom dresser, I noticed a bunch of small photographs, mostly of her kids and husband. One was a picture of Grandma when she was younger. She was standing next to a man, the same man in that picture I found in my dad's desk. He had to be my grandfather, Tom Collison.

Then I saw, in the back row of photos, a small, framed picture of a boy. It was a faded arcade picture, the kind you get when you sit in a booth, drop a dime in a slot, there's a flash, and out pops your picture. I picked it up and saw it was of one of those boys in the photos Dad had.

Why was his picture on my aunt's bureau? Was he Frank, Blaine, or Nelson Kasper?

I put the photo back, went into the kitchen. Aunt Betty was there alone, taking her lasagna out of her oven.

"Aunt Betty, can I ask . . ."

"Later, Pete . . . the birthday dinner is ready."

Dinner meant adults at one table, kids at another. No crossing over. Kids' talk was mostly baseball, a subject I usually loved, but tonight I hardly listened. I kept sneaking peeks at Dad, wondering who he was and what he had done.

Eventually the men started arguing politics. Dad sat there, saying little. He talked plenty of politics at home. Why didn't he talk here?

All of a sudden, Uncle Chris stood up and shouted, "You know what? You're all full of malarkey! When are you going to wake up to the truth? You're doomed. All of you!" He stalked away.

I'd seen him do that before. As usual, everybody just looked at him as if it didn't matter what he said and then resumed their arguments. I had no idea what Uncle Chris was talking about. He reminded me of Bobby.

The rest of the evening, I kept waiting for a chance to ask Aunt Betty about that picture, but I could never get to her alone. Between her fussing with food, her kids, and the birthday cake for Aunt Louise, she was always with someone or other.

Then, when I saw Uncle Chris sitting off alone, reading a newspaper, I decided to see if I could get him to tell me some family history. He and Bobby had become friends. Maybe he'd be friends with me, too. Besides, he had been yelling about the truth. I could use a bit of that.

Uncle Chris peeked at me from behind his paper, something called *The Daily Worker.*

"Hey, Pete," he called, "how you doing?"

"Okay."

"I heard you got suspended from school for fighting."

"Who told you?"

"Your brother. Glad you're a fighter like me."

"What do you mean?"

"Fighting—struggle—it's what the working class is all about." He held out his hands. He was older than Grandma, and his hands were big and solid, with thick fingers. "I work with my hands," he said. "Dirty hands. Not like your dad, one of those wishy-washy socialists."

He said "socialists" as if it was some girly thing. Not sure how to react, I just stood there.

He grinned, stood, rolled up his paper, and bopped my head. He towered over me. "Just kidding," he said. "Hey, like cars?"

"Sort of."

"I got a new one. Want to see it? Come on. I'm tired of my relatives. The car's parked right around the corner."

When we got down to the street, I said, "Can I ask you something about our family?" It was growing dark, and streetlights were already on.

"Ha! You've come to the right place. I know where the bodies are buried." He grinned. "Digging up dirt. It's what plumbers do."

I said, "What happened to my grandfather?"

He wheeled around. "Is that why you got me out here?" he demanded. "To ask me that?"

"You said you wanted—"

"How come you're asking?"

The best I could come up with was, "Grandma told me my grandpa vanished. Dad said he died."

Uncle Chris glared at me. "My brother disappeared."

"Where did he go?"

Chris stood there, breathing heavily, his big hands in fists. In the gloom, he looked enormous, a little scary. "Let me tell you something, Pete. Back in them days, there was the worldwide collapse of capitalism. Wasn't easy for your grandma to feed the kids when your grandfather, my brother, ran off. My nieces had to drop out of school, find what work they could. Everybody was just scrambling to keep alive. Eventually, I had to step in. It was me who kept the family together."

That was what Grandma said she had done. She hadn't mentioned Chris at all.

He kept going. "Did your dad help? No siree bob. Denny-boy stayed in school. Kept his nose in a book."

That time he said *book* as if it was a dirty word.

"After your grandfather went off, I was a second father to your dad. Tried to give him advice. Did he listen? No. After all I done for him, he announces he's going to take care of himself. Then he abandons his mother.

"Your dad had a friend. What was his name? Alberto Depaco. Dumb Al. From the old neighborhood. They went to the same high school and they ups and took off together. I tried to find Dennis for his mother's sake. If I had gotten to him, I would have belted him for a home run. I tried to find Tom, too."

He went on, angrier every moment. "Wasn't till after Pearl Harbor your father comes back. He's in the army. Married. With kids. Home for a couple of days, then off to the war. Near the end, he's wounded and suddenly Dennis is a different guy. Willing to be part of the family. Oh, sure.

"I'm a nice guy, so I offers to take him into my business. Be like my son. He tells me he wants to do something better. Ha! Better than me. Becomes a college professor. So here he is. A stuffed shirt. Thinks he's smarter than us all."

Chris was describing someone I didn't know. Dad wasn't like that.

"You want facts?" he went on. "Your old man thinks he's better than the rest of us. Professor I-do-what-I-want-the-heck-with-the-family. Some professor. Your father can't handle the truth. Can you?" He grabbed my arm, yanked me toward him, put his hot face and breath up close.

"I . . . I think so," I said, scared.

"Let me tell you something about myself, Pete. I'm a Communist. A real one. Proud of it."

I couldn't believe what he was saying.

"Because I know what's the truth. The future. I don't give up. Not like your father." He snorted. "Take it from me, Dennis is a turncoat."

He shoved me away. "Now go back to your aunt's and tell your old man to stuff it. I'm going to unclog a toilet. Clean work." With that, he turned and marched off.

Shaken, I watched him storm away, unable to make sense of what he said. *The future.* Hadn't Bobby complained that he was the only one in the family who cared about that? As I hurried back to my aunt's apartment, I realized I never saw Chris's new car. And he hadn't told me what had happened to my grandfather, either.

I felt like I was looking through a kaleidoscope. Every turn I made, things changed: shape, color, and the connections between them. It's a strange world when you can't put names to the colors you're seeing.

For the rest of the evening I avoided the adults and stayed with my cousins, playing Monopoly. Between turns, I tried to make sense of what I'd heard. I couldn't.

Going home on the subway, Bobby gave me an elbow. "Dodgers beat the Giants again. Giants lost their last three to the Dodgers. That's eight losses straight. *Eight.* Still a Giants fan?"

"Yeah," I muttered.

"Loser."

Soon as we got home, Dad went into his office and started grading student papers.

I followed him. "Dad, can I ask you something?"

"Sure," he said, without stopping his work.

"Uncle Chris told me he's a Communist."

Dad swiveled around and looked at me. I tried to read his face but couldn't tell what was there: disgust or uneasiness. He took a deep breath, smoothed out his mustache with his thumb, and said, "If he wants to say that, he's a bigger fool than I thought. What made him tell you?"

"Just talking," I said, not wanting to tell Dad I was trying to find out about him. "He was reading a newspaper called *The Daily Worker.* What's that?"

"The Communist Party newspaper."

"Oh. Why is Uncle Chris so angry?"

"He's always angry. And a couple of years ago he got into serious trouble over taxes. Didn't pay or something."

"What happened to him?"

"I'm not sure. In that situation . . . if it's truly bad, people can go to jail. But most often, they make a deal with the government. You know, slowly pay back the money along with fines they owe. Chris didn't go to jail, so he must have worked something out. But he just got angrier."

I stood there. "Dad?"

"What?" He was exhausted.

"Grandma said when you were a kid you ran away from home. That true?"

I had taken him by surprise. He sat there for a few moments, then said, "What made her tell you that?"

I gave a shrug. "I asked her."

Dad sat there, as if he weren't sure how to respond. He flexed his bad arm. "You know what, Pal, I think I've told you enough about that time. Nothing but unhappy memories."

I was not going to be pushed off. "Grandma said memories are dead-end streets."

His eyes softened. "She may be right."

"Dad, you said you'd always tell me the truth."

"Pal, sometimes the truth is too complicated. Now, I have papers to grade." He turned back to his work.

No more talk. Or answers. Kat was right: Parents don't want kids to know the truth about them.

Where did my grandfather go?

Where did Dad go? What did he do?

The name Alberto Depaco stayed in my head. Uncle Chris said he took off with Dad. Must have been close friends. But I never heard Dad mention him.

I went to the kitchen and checked the phone books. It was in the Brooklyn book that I found

Depaco, Alberto   452 Diggs Avenue
TRiangle 5 3218

He hadn't vanished.

Which meant I might get some answers from him. If I had the nerve. If I really wanted to be a hard-boiled detective.

And I did.

Monday morning, I met Kat by the newsstand. The first thing she said was, "Did your grandma tell you anything?"

"Said my grandfather vanished. Then my father vanished."

"Sounds like a magic show. Where'd they go?"

"Dunno."

"Why doesn't your father tell you?"

"Dunno."

"Just say 'doughnut.' It would sound better."

From there, the rest of the week had its ups and downs.

It was a good baseball week. It started out with the first night game of the season, when the Giants beat the Dodgers. I stayed up listening, relaying every good thing the Giants did to Bobby until he told me to shut up. After that game the Giants went on to beat the Cubs.

In school, it was mostly bad. Not only did we have another atomic attack drill, Suzy Russell passed out invitations for a Saturday-night birthday party. The whole class was invited. Except me.

But each day Kat and I had time to talk when we walked to and from school.

I told her about Al Depaco. Ten, fifteen times, I looked up his name in our Brooklyn phone book. Twice that week I even called his number. The first time was on Monday. When I got home from school, I grabbed the phone before I could tell myself not to and dialed. No answer. On Tuesday night, I called when everybody was out of the kitchen. It rang four times before a man's gravelly voice said "Hello."

I lost my nerve and hung up. More soft-boiled than hard-boiled.

"We need to go see that Al Depaco," I said to Kat on Wednesday.

"When?" she said.

"Some Saturday morning. Instead of the library."

She said, "Doughnut."

"This weekend, at the library, we can find out how to get where he lives. Come up with a plan."

That day after school, when I got into our building, I checked the lobby table for mail. There was something for my dad and a tan envelope for me.

I tore the envelope open and there it was, my Secret Code Maker. It was made of cardboard, about six inches long, four inches wide. At the top, in bold letters it read

SHREDDED WHEAT SECRET CODE MAKER

It was a simple thing. By shifting the letters of the alphabet, you could create a *new* alphabet. A could become B, then B would become C, and so on. That was code 1. In code 2, A became C, B became D. Shift again, new code, new code number. If I sent a coded message to Kat, and told her what code number I used, she could decode my message.

At first, I was excited. We had had schemes for leaving secret messages around the neighborhood. When we first learned about the Code Maker, it seemed the biggest thing in the world. That was before all this stuff happened. So I just flipped the Code Maker onto my desk and told myself to forget about it. My life already had too many real secrets.

On Thursday, as usual, I went to Mr. Ordson's. We began the way we always did, with me sitting at his small table, drinking milk, eating Oreos. He said, "Are things better in school?"

"Not really."

"I'm very sorry to hear that." He clasped his hands and touched his fingertips to his lips. After a long moment, he said, "I don't believe I ever told you how I lost my sight, did I?"

"No, sir."

"I was a soldier during World War One. We suffered a German gas attack."

I stared at him. All I could say was, "Sorry."

"Thank you."

"Did it hurt?"

"For a long time, yes."

"Is it . . . bad not seeing?"

"I don't like it," he said. "Of course, these days my blindness is no longer painful. What hurts is not seeing the world. Then again, though my wife passed on some years ago, I see her in my dreams."

As he went on, Mr. Ordson seemed to change. His mask began to melt. His face came alive. He was happy one moment. Sad the next.

He told me where he was born: North Carolina. His first name: Jasper. How he lived after the war, which he said was hard. Getting married. Being a blind parent. What would it be like never to see your own kid?

He answered my unspoken question when he said, "You don't have to see someone to love them."

His daughter, grown and married, lived in Chicago. They talked every week.

"Many old friends aren't alive," he said. "I am. But I have new friends. Like you. I read with my fingers. You read to me. There's the radio. I don't think I'll have much use for television."

I kept looking at him. He was telling me amazing

stories. What was most amazing was that he was talking to *me*. He even called me his friend. No adult had ever called me that.

"Well," he said at last, "I have rattled on, haven't I? You must pardon me."

We sat there not talking for so long, Loki looked up and around, as if making sure we were still there.

At last, I said, "Do you really want to know why my school isn't good?"

"Only if you wish to tell me."

I hesitated, afraid that if I told Mr. Ordson the Commie stuff, he would fire me. I said, "Not sure I should say."

"That's perfectly acceptable," said Mr. Ordson. "You don't need to. Let's do the first newspaper."

I reached for it. Except now I wanted to tell him everything, wanted to share my puzzles with an adult.

"Mr. Ordson," I whispered, "I'd . . . I'd like to tell you what's been happening."

He folded his hands. "When a young man talks to an old man, it is always a gift."

I started talking. It was like prying the cap off a shaken-up bottle of pop. Everything bubbled out.

I began with all the school stuff. When that was said, I couldn't stop. Though I knew I wasn't supposed to, just as I told Kat, I told Mr. Ordson about Dad.

As I talked, Ordson kept his blank eyes aimed at me. Never said a word. I'm not sure he even moved.

I ended by saying, "Worst thing is Kat, my best friend. Her father said she can't be friends with me anymore. You know, the Commie stuff."

"What does she say about all that?"

"Says she's still my best friend."

"You are lucky to have such a friend."

"She's a Dodger fan."

"And you?"

"Giants."

"And I cheer the Yankees. Despite such deep loyalties, I suspect we can get along."

"Mr. Ordson, there's more."

"Yes?"

I hesitated a moment and then said, "I'm pretty sure there are things my dad doesn't want me to know. I found some photographs my father was hiding. Pictures of him as a kid with another kid I never heard anything about."

"Seems innocent."

"Yeah. And maybe it was the kid he ran away with. Except there was a picture of that same kid on my aunt's table. I don't know why she'd have a picture of my dad's friend. Dad told me he'd always tell me the truth. I don't think he is. He's hiding something. I'm sure he is. What if he did something really bad?"

Mr. Ordson sat quietly for a few moments and then said, "Man has unraveled the complexities of the atom and how to release its force." He smiled. "Yet nothing is more complex or explosive than families."

"I just want to help Dad."

"And the FBI agent came to see you a second time?"

"I know why, too. They think I know my dad's secrets."

Mr. Ordson pressed his hands together, and, like before, placed them so his fingertips touched his mouth. He sat there for quite some time.

Feeling more and more uneasy, I whispered, "Mr. Ordson, do you want me to leave?"

"Why should I?"

"The Commie stuff. It's not great, is it?"

"It's difficult. I do believe the Soviet Union is our enemy. I don't believe your father or you are enemies. Indeed, I think you are a fine young man. I'm inclined to believe that about your father, too."

Then I said, "Mr. Ordson, I . . . I don't know what to do."

"Why must you do something?"

"I want to find out who the informer is. Why Dad ran off. What happened to my grandfather."

"What good would it do to learn all that?"

"Dad said it might help if he knew who the informer was. And that other stuff, maybe it's connected. In detective stories, questions always are."

"You care for your father a great deal, don't you?"

"Yes, sir."

Mr. Ordson said, "Somewhere I recall reading that a parent's secret is the child's burden. But generally speaking, I believe it's always better to learn the truth."

For a moment, neither of us spoke.

I said, "I . . . had one idea . . ."

"Do share."

"The guy Dad ran away from home with—I think I found out where he is. He lives in Brooklyn. Maybe he could give me answers."

"Are you allowed on the subway alone?"

"Yes."

"Then consider going to see him. It will take courage, but you have that. First, however, I suggest you get more cookies and milk. We cannot live on the bread of friendship alone."

Friday morning I told Kat about what Mr. Ordson said, how he agreed I should go see that Al Depaco.

"I'll go with you," she said.

"We can plan when we meet at the library tomorrow."

"Okay."

The day ended with my learning that the Giants had started losing again. It didn't bother me much because the next day Kat and I would plan our trip to see Depaco. It was just like a detective story, when the private eye learns where the big clue is. It might be dangerous to grab it, but he has to.

On Saturday, I got to the library a little before nine. Kat hadn't arrived. Soon as the doors opened, I went in and headed for the front desk, glad to see the young librarian there.

"How can I help you?"

"I need to know how to get somewhere in Brooklyn." I showed her Al Depaco's address.

"That should be no problem," she said, getting up. "Let's go over here." When she added a crinkly-eyed smile, I decided Kat was right. She was nice.

She led me to a section labeled "Reference," and pulled out a book called *Brooklyn Street Maps*. After flipping through some pages, she put a finger down as if pinning a bug. "Here's where you're going."

"How do I get there?"

She pointed to a thick red line. "That's the BMT subway line. The address you want is near the Graham Avenue station. Then a bit of a walk. Doesn't look too hard."

"Thanks," I said.

I studied the map, writing down names of subway stations and streets. I was sure Kat and I could find it.

When Kat arrived an hour later, I was sort of reading a large book about old-time baseball players. Mostly I had been worried about Kat. Wasn't she coming? Had something happened?

She plopped down in the seat next to me. "You're late," I whispered.

"Sorry."

"Getting ready for Suzy's party?"

"Not going."

"How come?"

She shook her head.

I looked at her. Her face was dirty, as if she had climbed out of a hole. "You okay?"

"No."

"What is it?"

When she didn't answer, I said, "The librarian showed me how to get to Al Depaco's place. It's not hard."

"That's good." Her voice was flat.

"Yeah. Maybe he'll give me some answers. And . . . I want him to be the informer."

"How come?"

"Then I won't have to think it's Bobby."

She stayed quiet, resting her hands on the table, squeezing and rubbing them as if they hurt.

I said, "Something bad happened, right?"

She nodded.

"What?"

She wouldn't look at me. A tear slid down the side of her cheek. She took off her glasses and smeared the tear away. Another one came and she smudged that one too, leaving streak marks up and down her face so it seemed as if she was peering out from behind a cage.

"Tell me," I said.

She picked at a fingernail. "Remember last week when we were here, a red-haired lady made us keep quiet?"

"Yeah."

"And I told you it was my mother's friend. Well, she told my mother she saw me here. You know, not at the movies. And said I was with you."

I waited.

"My mother told my father." Another tear slid down her cheek. "He's . . . he's sending me away to a girls' boarding school."

"You serious?"

She nodded.

"Why?"

"He said you're not a good friend for me. You being a boy . . . and a Commie. He said, 'I don't know which is worse.' You don't know how suspicious he is."

"He's sending you away . . . because of *me*?"

She nodded.

"What did your mother say?"

An angry shrug. "Daddy's boss."

I felt sick. "Sorry," I managed to say.

"Sorry is a sorry word."

I thought desperately. "We could run away! Vanish! Like my father did. Like his father did."

She said nothing, just gave a little shake of her head.

"When . . . when you going?"

"Tomorrow."

"Tomorrow!"

More tears came. She had the saddest face I ever saw.

My chest felt as if it was stuffed with mud. "You're . . . my best friend," I whispered.

"Same."

After a while I said, "You ever get that Secret Code Maker?"

A small nod.

"We could send each other messages."

"Suppose."

"You have a place I can send them?"

"Don't know where I'm going."

"You have my address, right?"

She nodded again.

I felt angry. Helpless. Though it was a library and you were supposed to be quiet, I felt like screaming "It's not fair! It's not right!"

She stood up. "Gotta go. I snuck out. They don't know I'm here. I didn't want to leave without saying good-bye."

She took a couple of steps, turned back, slid her glasses up, and gave a little wave. "See ya."

"See you . . . angel."

Eyes widening behind her glasses, she offered a small smile, and said, "Catch you later, traitor." Then she turned and ran.

I watched until I couldn't see her anymore. Then I pulled that big baseball book close up to my face and pretended to read. I was crying.

K at's dad is sending her off to boarding school. Today."
I had been so upset I waited a whole day to tell my
parents the news about Kat. It was during Sunday breakfast. Bobby was still asleep.

"Was there any reason?" asked Dad.

I looked at him. "Her father doesn't want her to be my
friend. The Commie business."

"That's dreadful," cried Ma.

"Utterly ridiculous," said Dad.

Ma said, "Do you know where she's going?"

I shook my head.

Dad said, "She was—is—a wonderful friend."

"Maybe there were other reasons," said Ma.

"Like what?" I asked.

"Sometimes when parents aren't happily married, kids pay a price."

"Hate them," I said.

"Understood," said Dad, ruefully.

When I got to the newsstand Monday morning and Kat wasn't there, I knew she was truly gone. It was an awful moment.

But there were more bad things.

That Tuesday we were having our regular family dinner. First thing my brother said was, "Giants in last place." Then he told us how some teacher had told him how smart he was.

The list of people I hated was growing.

Ma asked Dad how his day was.

"Not good. Dr. Dolkart, head of the History Department, told me the FBI had been around asking questions about my political past."

I was sure it was Ewing.

Bobby cried, "That mean they know you were a Communist? They have no right to—"

Ma snapped, "Bobby, let your father talk."

Dad gave me an unhappy look, as if I had told Bobby. He didn't know Bobby had been snooping around and listening to our conversations.

Dad went on: "Dolkart let me know that if there was anything unsavory about my past, there might be problems at the college. They're concerned about bad publicity. The college will act to protect its reputation."

"And do what?" Bobby demanded.

Dad said, "Fire me."

"Can they do that?" I asked.

"We'll find out," said Dad.

"Tell them you hate Communists!" cried Bobby. "That what you did a long time ago was something stupid. That'll satisfy them."

Dad spoke sharply: "Bobby, I don't believe any government has the right to inquire about my beliefs."

I said, "Was the FBI agent who went to your college the same one who came here?"

"What FBI agent?" said Bobby. "How come no one tells me anything?"

Liar. I was sure he knew all about it.

"The FBI came around to question me," said Dad. "Pete happened to be here alone."

Dad's eyes shifted toward Ma for some secret talk. What he said was, "I just wanted you to know what might happen."

"Just tell the FBI you were stupid," my brother cried. "Otherwise you're going to ruin my life."

Ma turned to Bobby. "That's a rather self-centered way of thinking about this."

"If Dad gets into trouble with the government, I'll never get to go to that science camp. It's run by the government."

"This is about *all* our lives, Bobby," said Dad.

Bobby got red in the face and jumped up. "This family is so stupid," he said. He stormed off.

After a moment, Dad said to me, "Just know I won't get another teaching job. I'll be blacklisted."

I said, "Like Dashiell Hammett."

"Right," said Dad, standing. "Anyone want to listen to the radio? I need to relax."

I said, "Did you tell Bobby about the Commie stuff you told me?"

"No. I assumed you did," he said as he went toward the radio room. Ma went with him.

I stayed at the table, thinking. What Bobby said was the proof I needed. He had been snooping, listening, and faking that he didn't know about the FBI coming after Dad. Then I thought about what he had said, that the government could take him to the moon. The way I saw it, he'd do anything to go. Did he inform on Dad—make a deal with the government—so he could get to that camp?

Awful, but it fit.

I reminded myself—once again—that Dad told me *not* to talk about what was going on. But I couldn't keep it locked up. It was too big. So on Thursday, when I went for my usual time with Mr. Ordson, soon as I sat down at the table, I said, "Want to know what happened this week?"

"I should be pleased to listen."

"Kat's parents sent her away. Because of me. And now the FBI is asking questions about Dad at his college. He might lose his job. The more I work on it, the surer I am it's my brother who went to the FBI. He's the informer."

He said, "That's quite a lot of news for one week. I am terribly sorry about Kat. And your father. Now, Pete, do you truly believe your brother is working with the FBI against your father?"

"Told you, he's been snooping around, listening to conversations, looking in Dad's files."

He said, "How very sad, if true. Pete, there's an old saying: A brother who is a friend is the best of friends while a brother who is an enemy is the worst of enemies. Cain and Abel, alas. Can I tell you something as a friend, Pete?"

"Yeah."

"Regarding your brother, you need more evidence."

"I thought of that," I said. "Remember my telling you about an old friend of my father's? That Depaco guy? If he's the informer, I won't have to worry about my brother."

"Then the sooner you see him, the better."

"That's why I'm going on Saturday."

Saturday morning, I told my parents I was going to the movie show. Instead, I headed for the subway, the directions to Depaco's home in my pocket, Sam Spade in my head.

Leaving the sunlight behind, Pete Collison walked into the BMT Borough Hall station. He popped a dime into the turnstile slot and went down to the platform. The only light there came from dim bulbs in metal cages on the ceiling. The air was damp and reeked of trash and carried sounds of dripping water, creaking beams, and the far-off rumblings of trains. On the platform, most people were standing still, not looking at one another. Others walked about aimlessly, as if wondering if they were ever going to get anywhere.

Ten minutes later a train burst in like a rocket on wheels. Brakes shrieking, it lurched to a stop. Doors leaped open with a bang. People hurried off as if afraid they might be trapped. Pete jumped on and worked his way through the cars until he reached the first one. From behind the front window, he watched the tunnel whiz by like a movie about darkness, the train rocking and rumbling. Twenty minutes later, he got off at the Graham Avenue station and climbed to the street. The sun was still shining.

Right off, I could tell that this part of Brooklyn was different from where I lived. It was much more crowded and the crowd was more colorful, people's skin as well as their clothing. They were going in and out of small shops plastered with signs offering crayons to cabbage and everything in between. The air smelled of gas, trash, and food.

I found my way to a narrow street lined with tightly parked cars and skinny trees. In small fenced-in front yards lay broken flowerpots, bikes, dented garbage cans, and busted baby carriages. One yard had an American flag. Another had a few yellow daffodils. Through an open window, I heard a kid crying while someone sang a song in a language I had never heard till then.

The house with Depaco's number was an old two-story yellow brick building in a row of yellow brick buildings.

I waited until my heart stopped thumping, walked up the three cement steps, took a deep breath, and pushed the doorbell. The buzz inside sounded like a giant mosquito. Moments later, the door swung open.

Standing there was a thin guy wearing a sleeveless white undershirt. His deep, dark eyes peered down at Pete from under eyebrows that lay across his forehead like an iron bar. His long, swarthy face needed a shave. A gold chain lay high on his hairy chest, probably marking the low boundary for his razor. His knobby-toed feet were bare and a lit cigarette was wedged into one corner of his mouth like a lollypop stick that had lost its sweet.

"Yeah?" he said.

"Sir, are you Alberto Depaco?"

"What if I was?" His voice was thick, gravelly, and suspicious.

"My father is Dennis Collison."

His eyes got big. A grin crept across his face. "Dennis Collison? You gotta be kidding. Who are you?"

"His son. Pete Collison."

He snorted a horselaugh. "Holy moly. You look just like him. Jeez Louise! Dennis Collison. Son of a blue bucket. Been a billion years. He okay?"

"Yes, sir."

"Good old Dennis. What's he doing? What you doing here?"

"I wanted to ask you some things about my dad."

Beaming, Depaco pulled the door wide open. "Come on in. Pete, eh? Let me guess why he sent you," he giggled. "He needs me 'cause he's planning to rob another bank."

His words exploding in my ears, I managed to follow him into a room with a drooping couch, wide easy chair, and Philco TV. A shaggy gray rug lay on the floor. The walls were painted green, and one wall had a framed painting on velvet of a stag with big antlers standing in a forest. A low table had overflowing ashtrays shaped like yellow flowers. Flakes of gray cigarette ash dotted the table like sooty snow.

"Go on, kid, sit yourself down." He pointed to the couch. He dropped into the easy chair. Then he slapped both his knees and stared at me, his grin as big as a banana.

"How about that. Dennis Collison."

"Yes, sir." I kept staring at him, attempting to find a connection between him and my dad.

"Tell me again why you're here."

"Wanted to learn about my dad."

Depaco laughed. "You come to the right guy. Back in them days your dad and me, we was like this." He held up a hand with crossed fingers. "Best of chums. Maybe because we were so different. Mutt and Jeff for real. Right here in Brooklyn."

Almost afraid to ask, I said, "Did . . . did he really rob a bank?"

Depaco laughed as if that was the best joke on *Can You Top This?* "Naw. But, I'm telling you, we thought about it.

So broke, we'd do anything. Hey, them days, you ran on empty but dreamed on full."

I just sat there, staring at him.

"Sometimes, guess how we'd get food. Way past midnight, back behind restaurants, we'd go through garbage cans and boxes of trash. You wouldn't believe what we found. Once, a live lobster." He cracked up again. "What do you do with a live lobster? We put him in the East River. Probably still there."

The image of my father going through garbage was beyond me.

"But Dennis—your father—he had dreams. Real ones. He was as smart as a starched collar."

I said, "Did you know him when he left home?"

Depaco grinned. "Know him? Hey, him and me, we done it together." He laughed again, as if that too was a joke. "Back then, with times so hard, better for your family if you left. Parents couldn't feed you. So guys took off. To California. Hobo camps. Conservation Corps.

"Me," he said, "my parents asked me to leave. Nothing mean. My ma cried. So did my old man. Hey, me too. God bless 'em. I was helping by going."

"Do you know anything about my father's father?"

"That was the thing. See, when Tom disappeared, your dad's ma and his Uncle Chris made your old man drop out of school and look for work, which there was none. Hey, his mother wouldn't even let him keep no books."

I must have looked astonished.

"It's true," he said. "Fact, Dennis used to give me his books so as to hide 'em from his family."

"Why?"

"His ma said reading and school was snobby. For the rich. Didn't want him to be no different from his family. She still alive?"

I nodded.

"Toughest turkey on the track. Oh, and your dad's uncle was always giving Dennis head bonks. He was poison to Dennis. I always thought he was jealous of your dad for being so smart.

"'I'll give you smarts,' he'd say. And he'd belt your old man. Whack! Whack! I mean, mean. 'Be like the rest of us,' he kept telling your dad."

I remembered how Uncle Chris had been on the street, when I thought he was about to hit me.

"Them two hated each other," Depaco went on. "But see, with your dad's pop gone, Chris was the big man on campus. So your dad and I run off."

"Where'd you go?"

"Your old man and me, we put together a shack with wood and cardboard by the East River. It's what people did. What else was they going to do? Made whole villages. Called 'em Hoovervilles. I'm telling you, we weren't the only kids.

"Your dad gets into some Manhattan high school. He gets a night job cleaning toilets in subway stations. Can't get worse than that, but hey, he's lucky to get it. Me, I was delivering messages around town for tips.

"Hey, listen to this. Your father loved playing check-ers. But we don't have a board. One day he finds this bottle of aspirin in one of those stations. He takes the pills, smudges some with soot, draws lines on the floor of our shack for a checkerboard and we played. With aspirin pills! Course, he always beat me."

He laughed until a cigarette cough made him stop.

I said, "What happened to my dad's father?"

"No idea. All Dennis told me is, his father found work somewhere."

"You don't know where?"

"Listen, guys was so desperate for work, they'd go any-where. What's your dad doing now?"

"He's a college professor."

"Jeez Louise." Depaco laughed with delight. "Love it. Your dad was always saying, 'I'm going to be different than my family.' And he done it.

"Good for him. Me—nothing like that. But I get along. Decent factory job. Union wages. Family. Couple of nice kids. Hey, your father know you were coming to see me?"

I shook my head.

"How'd you even find out about me?"

"Uncle Chris."

"You kidding? It's Chris that drove me and your dad apart. Okay, your dad and me was sharing that shack, a month, maybe two, scrambling. One night Chris shows up all nasty and mean, looking for Dennis with a belt in his hands. Good thing your dad was working.

"Chris tells me he's coming back to grab your dad. When Dennis comes home, I tell him. Your dad hears, he takes off. Gone like 'Quick-Henry-the-Flit.' I never saw him again."

"How old was Dad?"

"Nineteen, twenty."

"Did my dad do political things?"

"Like what?"

"Join . . . Communist stuff."

"Hey, those days, we all talked wild. Understand? People used to say, 'Got nothing, think anything.' But nah, Dennis didn't do nothing red I ever heard. All he wanted was to stay in school and get smarter."

"Did the FBI ever talk to you about him?"

Depaco was startled. "FBI? Why should they? Hey, you telling me he did rob a bank?" He laughed again. "I'm guessing your dad didn't tell you much about those times, right?"

I shook my head.

He shrugged. "Hey, who wants to remember what's better to forget?"

Depaco asked me questions about my father, if he had been in the war, what he taught, about my mother, about my family.

But by then I was sure he wasn't the informer. I stood up. "I have to go," I said.

"Sure, sure." He shook my hand with two hands and walked me to the door. "Hey, tell Dennis I'd love to see him. If he wants to, is all. Maybe him being a college professor, he won't. But, let me tell you, him and me, we could talk old times both ways backwards and upside down. Yeah, tell him to come around."

I went out the door and down his steps.

Then, as I turned to wave good-bye, Depaco called, "Hey, Pete. Just remembered something. Back then, just before your dad took off, he found out what Frank was doing. Not that he told me, but what I'm thinking, maybe he went after him. Or the two of them went off. But it's so long ago so I'm not sure I got that right."

"Frank?"

"Yeah, you know. His brother, Frank."

Waving good-bye, he shut the door.

Staggered, I walked away, my head spinning. What Depaco had described seemed like another universe. And now . . . a brother?

At least I understood why Dad left home. But—where did he go after being with Depaco? What did he do? And I still didn't know what happened to my grandfather.

But *Frank* was the biggest thing. That name was on the picture. Did Dad really have a brother? Was *he* the kid in the photo? Why would Dad's brother be a secret?

Okay: Depaco wasn't the informer. Which meant it had to be Bobby. *My* brother.

It was a long ride back home. At one point, I could have sworn a man I had seen on the way to Depaco's was also on my return train. Was I being followed again?

I told myself not to be stupid. Stick with the facts.

That afternoon, Dad was in his office, writing. Ma was in the kitchen, slicing beets. I had no idea where Bobby was.

I wandered into the kitchen, picked up an apple from a bowl. "Can I ask you something?" I asked.

"Of course."

"Grandma told me about Dad's dad."

She stopped working. "Oh? What did she say?" She didn't say it to me, but to the air in front of her.

"Grandma said he vanished a long time ago. Dad said he died. Which was it?"

Ma studied her hands, as if just noticing they were stained red by beets. "I didn't know your father then."

"*Did* my grandfather die?"

Speaking carefully, she said, "That's my understanding."

"Grandma told me Dad ran away from home. How come? Where'd he go? What did he do?"

Ma took a deep breath, turned toward me, and said, "You need to ask your father."

"He won't tell me."

Ma stood there. I was sure she was trying to decide what to tell me. Finally, she said, "In his last year of high school he won a scholarship to Indiana University. That's where I met him."

"I heard he ran away before he finished high school."

"Perhaps I don't have my dates right. It was a long time ago." She went back to the beets.

Not believing her—she remembered every aunt's and uncle's and cousin's birthday, on both sides of the family—I said: "What about Dad having a . . . brother?"

She stood very still. "Who told you that?" she asked.

"Is there a brother?"

"Pete, you really need to ask your dad these questions."

"I told you, he won't answer."

Ma went back to working.

"Ma . . ."

"Please talk to him."

I could have asked Dad, but sure he would lie to me again, I tossed my apple core into the garbage can and walked away. I had to find another way to get answers from Dad. Took a few days, but I worked out a plan.

On Wednesday, the Dodgers were in first place, Giants

in sixth. When I got home after school, no one was there, as usual. I went to the kitchen and checked Dad's work number, which was on the fridge door.

He'd been staying late at his office Wednesday afternoons, because—he told us—he could talk to students who might drop in.

Sure Dad wouldn't answer direct questions, my plan was to call him at work, which I rarely did, and tell him I had something I needed to talk to him about when he got home. He'd ask what, I'd just say, "Your brother, Frank," and hang up. That would give him time to work out an answer by the time he got home.

I dialed his number. The office secretary picked up on the second ring.

"History Department. May I help you?"

"This is Pete Collison. My dad is Dennis Collison. Can I talk to him, please?"

The woman said, "Oh, hi, Pete. Your father just left. It's Wednesday. He's at the gym."

"Gym?"

"That's where he goes on Wednesday afternoons."

"I thought he was seeing students."

"That's Tuesday mornings. If he comes back, shall I have him call you?"

"No, thanks," I said.

I put the phone down and tried to make sense of what I heard. Never, not once, did Dad say he was going to a gym. With his war arm, he didn't do things like that.

Where was he going?

I was in my room when my mother came home and poked her head in. "Hi, honey. How was your day?"

I said, "Hey, Ma, when I got home from school I called Dad. He wasn't there."

She smiled. "He has so many meetings."

"The lady I spoke to said he always goes to a gym on Wednesday afternoons."

She took a moment to reply. "She must have confused him with someone else. Or maybe you misunderstood her."

"That's what she said."

Her smile faded. "Ask your father when he comes home," she said, and walked down the hall.

I was sure she knew where Dad went. I was also sure she'd tell him that I asked. I decided to wait and see what he'd say to me about it.

Dad said nothing. Not at dinner. Not after dinner. Not a word.

Next day after school, I went to Mr. Ordson's. As Mario, the doorman, held the door open for me, he said, "Hey, Pete, somebody was asking me why you're always coming here."

That stopped me. "Who?"

"Don't know. Some guy."

"What did he look like?" I asked.

"I was helping Mrs. Lyons with her shopping bags. Wasn't paying attention."

"What did you tell him?"

He shrugged. "That you work for 4B."

"Thanks," I said, heading for the elevator. I was sure it had been Ewing.

Once in Mr. Ordson's place, I sat down at his table. "I never told you because I had to think things out, but I went to my father's old friend, that Mr. Depaco."

"Good for you. What did you learn?"

"He told me lots. And I'm sure he isn't the informer."

"Why?"

"He didn't know my father was a Communist."

"Did you gather further clues?"

"I know why Dad left home." I told Mr. Ordson about Uncle Chris and my grandmother. "But the big thing Depaco said was that my father had a brother. Said his name was Frank."

"Is that important?"

"Mr. Ordson, no one in the family ever mentions him."

"*Never?*"

"Nope."

"How singular."

"Dad had a photograph of two boys hidden in his file. On the back of the picture were three names: Frank, Nelson Kasper, Blaine. My Aunt Betty has a photo of one of the boys on her bureau. I think it's this Frank. No idea who Nelson Kasper or Blaine are."

"You've become quite the detective."

"I guess," I said, pleased.

Mr. Ordson steepled his fingers in front of his mouth and then said, "Pete, have you considered the possibility that your father's father did die? That this so-called brother is something Mr. Depaco got mixed up? You told me it's been years since he and your father were together.

"You also say no one in your family mentions a brother. Most likely it is because he does not exist.

"Most importantly, have you considered that there is no informer, and that the FBI learned about your father on their own? That is part of their duties."

"Dad told me they talked to him."

"Well, yes—"

"They wouldn't have talked to him if they hadn't been tipped off. I'm sure that's how this all began. And they think I know what Dad won't tell them. That's why they keep coming after me. Just now, Mario said someone asked him why I was always coming here. I bet it was the FBI guy."

Ordson smiled and shook his head. "I have very nosey neighbors."

"Mr. Ordson, yesterday I called my dad's office to ask him about Frank. The secretary told me he goes to a gym every Wednesday."

"Is that of interest?"

"My dad never said he was going to a gym. See, he's got a bad arm. From the war. He doesn't do stuff like that. But that secretary said he goes *every* Wednesday. He must be going *somewhere*. When I asked my mother about it, she said she didn't know. I don't believe her.

"Mr. Ordson, do you think it'd be wrong if I went to my dad's office and tailed him next Wednesday? Find out where he's going?"

He frowned. "Pete, you need to respect your father."

"But he doesn't tell the truth. One minute I think I figure things out. Next minute I learn something that makes me see it's wrong. It's like a detective story that doesn't stop. I have to solve the mystery."

Mr. Ordson was quiet for a few moments, then he said, "I fear that in an age of suspicion the last people we suspect is ourselves. Tell me, Pete, is there anyone about whom you're not suspicious?"

"Kat. You."

"Kat is gone. That leaves just me. Therefore, I must consider your question thoughtfully. Now, let's get to the papers."

The rest of the afternoon went on as usual until Mr. Ordson was letting me out the front door. "Pete, I urge you to ask your father directly about this so-called brother. And going to the gym. Perhaps there is an easy explanation for both."

"What if he lies?" I said. "Or just goes silent the way he's been doing? Something is cockeyed."

"Think very carefully before you do something you might regret."

"Mr. Ordson, I have to know what's going on."

"Do me this one favor, Pete. Promise me that if you decide to follow your father next Wednesday—you have my number—you'll call me first."

"Why?"

"Friends talk over important decisions. Will you?"

"Well, . . . okay."

"Thank you." He shut the door.

I would call Mr. Ordson, but I had already made up my mind. I was going to follow Dad.

R ain on Saturday is worse than rain on weekdays. I had
stopped going to movies. I had no friends at school.
Kat was gone. I had no place to go. Around noon, Ma
came into my room and handed me an envelope. "Mail
for you."

I looked at the return address:

Blessed Saint Anne's School for Girls
Westport, Connecticut

I tore open the envelope and read the page it contained:

6

XYUL NLUCNIL C BUNY CN

BYLY GCMM SIO XIXAYLM QLCNY E

It was a secret message from Kat.

I ransacked my desk, found the Secret Code Maker and decoded her letter.

dear traitor i hate it here miss you dodgers write k

In code, I wrote back:

miss you too my dad had a secret brother working on clues donavan is the dumps giants p

I hadn't felt so happy in a long time.

That Monday, May 28, the Giants' Willie Mays, their nineteen-year-old rookie, got his first hit, a home run. I wished when Dad was nineteen he had done that instead of becoming a Communist.

At dinner that night, Ma had served the food but hadn't asked her usual "How were things at school?" question, when Dad said, "I have something important to share."

We looked at him.

He said, "At the college today, I received a special-delivery letter—a subpoena. That's a legal summons informing me that I've been called to testify, July 14th, before the Subversive Activities Control Board."

My heart sank.

"What's that?" asked Bobby.

"It's a congressional committee that investigates what the government calls Communist 'fronts,' groups the government thinks have been infiltrated by Communists. Or individuals they think are subversive."

"You going to be sent to one of those camps?" I asked.

"Why did they call you?" Bobby shoved in. For once, he didn't smirk. He looked upset.

"They've ordered me to provide information. Under the McCarran Act, they can do that."

Bobby said, "You were just a teenager then."

Dad said, "That's true. And a long time ago. I'm just telling you what's happened. Don't forget, I'm hardly the only one being called. Lots of others. Teachers. Union leaders. Writers. Actors. Whoever they want."

"Do you have to go?" I said.

"Yes," said Dad, flicking some eye talk at Ma.

"What will that committee do?"

"They will question me. If they really know my history, I can't believe they're truly interested in me. My guess is they want me to give information about other people. Ask me to name people who I think are Communists or left-wingers."

Looking at Bobby, I said, "You mean, be an informer?"

"That's one way to put it."

"Just tell them what they want to know," cried Bobby. "Those people aren't your problem."

"It's not so easy," said Dad. "I thought I told you, I don't think the government should question me about my beliefs. Or people I knew. I won't stoop so low as to tell them what other people think."

"Just tell them you're sorry," said my brother, getting more and more upset. He looked as if he were about to cry. "It's not worth it," he cried. "Just apologize!"

Dad, ignoring him, said, "What you all need to know is there's a good likelihood I'll lose my job at the college. I doubt the college will want to have a former Communist on their faculty."

"Tell them you were just a kid," said Bobby. "You said you didn't do anything."

"That doesn't seem to matter these days," said Dad.

"What'll happen with my summer camp?" said Bobby.

"Hopefully, nothing," Dad answered.

"But—" began Bobby.

I cut him off, "Why don't you try to stop thinking only about yourself."

Bobby didn't snap back. He just sat there, looking miserable.

Back at my desk I couldn't do homework. I thought about Dad, how he might lose his job and what would happen to us. What would Dad say when that committee asked him questions? I thought about Bobby, too. How upset he was with Dad's news. Maybe he wasn't the informer. Maybe if I asked him straight out I'd get a straight answer.

"Hey, Bobby?" I called. "I need to ask you—"

"Shut up," he said, cutting me off. "I've got to study. I need an A in everything from here on."

"I just—"

"Hey, put an egg in your shoe and beat it."

I backed off. He was never going to help. As always, I was on my own.

The next day, Tuesday, the Dodgers were in first place. The Giants were fifth. After school, I went straight home. About four thirty, I was in the kitchen when the phone rang. I picked it up. "Hello?"

"Who's this?" said someone, a man's voice.

On the alert, I said, "Pete."

"Hey, Pete. Uncle Chris."

"Oh, hi," I said, wondering if he could hear my dislike of him.

"Your dad there?"

"Still at work."

"Wanted to tell him Grandma is a little under the weather. Nothing serious. Just he should know. Tell him I called."

"Okay."

He was silent for a moment, and then he said, "I should apologize for losing my temper the other day. Listening to your uncles talk baloney turns up my steam."

"Okay."

"Let me make it up to you. Come out to my shop in Coney Island. I'll show you around. We'll have a good time."

Wanting nothing to do with him, all I could think of saying was, "Maybe."

"Hey, come on over tomorrow, after school. I'll treat you to a hot dog at Nathan's."

Fishing for an excuse, I said, "Going to see my dad tomorrow."

"Tomorrow? At his college?"

"Uh-huh."

"How come?"

"Want to," I said, annoyed that he would even ask.

"That's nice. Some other time, then. Hey, tell Dennis I called."

"I will."

I hung up. Telling Chris I was going to Dad's college the next day, when Dad supposedly went to the gym, made my plan to follow him real. Then I remembered about calling Mr. Ordson. I didn't want to. Still, I had promised and he was my only friend. I picked up the phone again.

"This is Jasper Ordson."

"Mr. Ordson, it's Pete."

"Hello, Pete. How are you?"

"Fine. I'm going to do that . . . you know."

"Follow your father?"

"Yes."

"As your friend, Pete, I urge you not to."

"I have to."

"Is there nothing I can say to discourage you?"

I didn't even answer.

"Well, then, I admit I'll be interested in what happens. I'll expect you Thursday."

"Okay."

On Wednesday, right after school, I grabbed Ma's newspaper, got home, and dumped my books on my bed.

"Hey," Bobby called from his side.

That stopped me. "How come you're home?" I said.

"Big exam tomorrow. Told you, got to study."

"See you," I called.

"Where you going?"

He was the last person I'd tell where I was headed. "See you later!"

On the street, I looked back up at our apartment. Bobby was staring down at me from my parents' room, but he could have no idea where I was going. I headed for the subway and Dad. I was excited. This was real detective stuff.

29

*N*ew City College was in Manhattan, a bunch of large, square buildings that reminded Pete of a cemetery with giant tombstones. His father's office was in the Spencer Center, the name chiseled in stone over the entryway. The entryway consisted of a row of wooden doors with doorknobs that looked like baked potatoes. In front of the building was a piebald patch of grass, stunted trees, and hard iron benches. Students—mostly pale young men—were sitting, standing around, reading, and talking, as if they had nowhere else to go. But there were signs everywhere pointing out where to hide in case Communists dropped an atom bomb.

I found a bench off to one side so I could keep my eyes on the entrance. Anytime I had been there with Dad, he had used those wooden doors.

I didn't have to wait long. Dad came out the one on the far left. In his hand was a leather briefcase, and on his head, his brown hat. I let him go by and then started to follow.

Leaving the college campus, he walked along city streets, heading west. He went without hesitation, never looking back in my direction. I kept a half block behind. Maybe he *was* going to a gym. I didn't think so, but I almost hoped so.

After a while, the neighborhood began to change. Buildings weren't so big. There were fewer offices. We went by a school. A church. Private homes. I saw more kids around.

Dad kept going.

When he reached Hudson Street, he crossed over, made a left turn, and headed south. I stepped into the street between a truck and a car in the middle of the block. When I peeked out from behind the truck, I saw a fast-moving car coming down the street. It was a black Ford, with a license plate that read

PED459.

My heart lurched. Ewing was following me.

I jumped back, stooped low, and stayed down, hoping

he didn't see me. At the end of the street the car stopped. Ewing sprang out and looked around.

After a few moments, he got back into his car. The door slammed, the car started up, reached the corner, and turned north.

I guessed he was going to circle the block and come back to see where I'd gone. As soon as he was out of sight, I ran south along Hudson Street, the way Dad had gone.

That's when a whole new thought bolted into my brain. My first notion had been that Ewing was following me this afternoon. But what if it was Dad he was really after? What if I had led him straight to the secret place Dad was going?

Still going south, I kept a lookout for Dad's hat. When I caught sight of it, he was far ahead, going at his steady pace.

I glanced back over my shoulder. Ewing's black Ford reappeared at the corner and was now coming in my direction. Up ahead, Dad was going into a building.

I quick-stepped onto the street and hoped Ewing was looking at me, like a decoy. Then I got back on the sidewalk and dashed past the building Dad had entered. When I reached the corner, I looked back.

In front of the building Dad had gone into was a "Loading Only—No Parking" area. The black Ford pulled into that space and stopped. Was Ewing coming for me or going after Dad?

I stood in the open, watching.

Ewing got out of the car and started walking toward me. Hands cupped round his mouth, he bellowed, "Hey, Pete, wait! I really want to talk."

I ran down a side street. At the first building, a paint store, I yanked open the plate-glass door and ran inside, then stood by the entrance and peered out.

Moments later, the Ford cruised slowly down the street. I could see Ewing scanning the sidewalks. He went by me. But he might have seen Dad go inside that building, and if he was after Dad, I needed to give a warning. Still, if I warned my dad, he would know I had trailed him. Not good. Yet if something bad happened, it would be worse. Plus, the whole point of my following Dad was to learn what he was doing.

Back on the sidewalk, I looked right and left. Seeing no sign of Ewing, I returned to Hudson Street. I reached the corner, checked again. Nothing. I turned north and didn't stop until I was standing across from the building Dad had gone into.

There was a sign by its entrance: Duffy Nursing Home. That surprised me. But knowing it wasn't a gym made me feel better about following Dad.

The front of the Duffy Nursing Home was brick painted white, much of that paint peeling. Its pebbled glass door had a small crack in one corner. Each of the four stories had twenty windows across, shades drawn down at different levels, making it look like a patient's fever chart. At the top of the building was a stone slab with "1910" painted on it. The zero was only half there—like a smile painted by mistake. The building was in need of some of its own nursing.

I shot across the street, ran up about twelve steps, pulled the door open, and stepped into a lobby.

It was a big, empty area, as quiet as three a.m. Old blue carpeting covered the floor. Overhead, bars of fluorescent lights flickered. Against one wall stood two large leather chairs, one leaking what looked like a dirty cloud. There was also a leather couch with no pillows, a half-empty water cooler with bluish water, and a hat stand with no hats. A low table held some old, tattered magazines, Life, Look, *and* The Saturday Evening Post. *On one wall hung a photograph of snow-covered mountains, taken by someone who probably wanted to be as far from this place as possible.*

A lady sat behind a reception desk. Her blond hair didn't match her wrinkled face. Her lips were bright red, and her eyebrows were mostly pencil. If you asked me, she had made herself look older by trying to make herself look younger. She glared at me with a face that said I shouldn't be there. But her lips said, "May I help you?"

"I'm supposed to meet my father here. Professor Collison."

"And you are?"

"His son, Pete."

Her face softened. "Oh, yes," she said, as if she knew the name. "Do you know where to go?"

I shook my head.

"That hallway. Last room on the right."

"Thank you."

Pete walked down a wide hall. Everything was white: walls, ceiling, and floor. The linoleum was so white it seemed illegal to walk on it. An old man was slowly pushing a wheelchair that held an even older man dressed in a white gown, his white-haired head tipped forward like a wilted white flower. Every few feet were white doors, some open. Inside the rooms were beds with white frames and white blankets. In one, an old man was propped up beneath the blankets, wearing white pajamas, his face blank. Outside another, two old ladies were whispering in tense voices to a young woman dressed in white, right down to her shoes. The only color came from a sign at the end of the hallway: in letters the color of blood, it read EXIT.

I came to the last room on the right and peeked in. An old man lay on the bed, propped against a stack of white pillows. His face was thin and wrinkled, with hollow cheeks and closed eyes. Gray-white hair hung down on both sides of his face, like curtains parting. Or maybe they were closing.

On the bed was a checkerboard, the pieces set up to play. Next to the bed, someone was sitting in a chair, his back to me. Dad. He had no idea I was in the doorway, standing behind him, watching.

The more I stared at the man in the bed the more familiar he seemed. Then Dad began to get up.

I jumped from the doorway, scooted to the door under the EXIT sign, and pushed my way through. I ran down a short flight of stairs, found another door. It opened into an alley. At the end of the alley was the regular street. I was there in seconds.

Seeing no trace of Ewing's car, I ran north for a couple of blocks, then headed east, and eventually got to West Fourth Street and took the A train to Brooklyn.

As the subway roared through the dark tunnels, I couldn't stop thinking about that old man my dad was visiting. I was sure I had seen his face somewhere. Gradually, an idea began to form, an impossible idea: I had seen Dad's dad. My grandfather.

I went right to the kitchen. Ma was sitting there, reading her newspaper. She looked up and smiled. "Hello, love. How was your day?"

"Fine. Bobby home? Dad?"

"Bobby's in his room. Dad should be soon."

She bent over her paper.

I scooted into Dad's office, pulled open the file cabinet, yanked out the "Frank" folder, and checked the picture of the man and two kids. Okay. One of the kids was definitely Dad. He had his arm around the other, younger kid. Had to be Dad's brother, Frank. But who were Nelson Kasper or Blaine, the names written in pencil? And "2573." What did that mean? Was it some code? Despite all my detective work, I had no idea.

I checked the little picture, too, the one with Grandma Sally, my dad, his sisters, and the other boy, who I was now sure was Dad's brother.

There was also a man in both pictures. I stared at him. Before, I thought he was Uncle Chris. Now I was positive it was Dad's dad, the guy in that nursing home. Where had he come from? Why was it all such a big secret?

I fled to my room. Good thing too, because ten minutes later, Dad got home. Standing in the doorway to my room he said, "Hey, Pal, have a good day?"

"Not bad," I said, which was as true as Santa Claus. I wasn't going to say anything about what I had discovered. I had too many unanswered questions.

Dinner was normal, except far as I was concerned I couldn't help feeling as if an extra person was at the table: Dad's dad, invisible to everybody except me.

After dinner, I retreated to my room and tried to do homework. Bobby came and stood behind me. "What's digging you?"

"Nothing."

"Something's bothering you. You sat there at dinner like a dead street pigeon."

"When I went out this afternoon, you were watching me from the window."

"So what?"

"Why were you watching?"

"Why not?"

After a moment I said, "Do you know what happened to Dad's father?"

Bobby stood there like a stopped clock.

I said to him, "I just want to know what you know."

"How about you putting your question in a can and flushing it."

I said, "When I asked Grandma, she said Dad's dad vanished. Dad said he died."

"Want some advice? Don't stick your nose into other people's business."

I took a wild shot. "Why? It going to keep you from going to the moon?"

Bobby's mouth hung open. "Shut up!" he shouted. "You don't know what you're talking about!" He stormed over to his side. I heard him drop onto his bed.

I went and looked at him. He was lying with his back toward me. "Get out of here!" he cried.

I headed for the kitchen. As I passed Dad's office, he called out, "Hey, Pal."

All these secrets made it hard for me to look at him, as if he might see what I knew on my face.

He said, "You love *The Maltese Falcon*. A few years ago, they made a terrific movie of it with Humphrey Bogart as Sam Spade. It's going to be shown at my college's Film Society in a couple of weeks. I thought we could go."

"Sure," I said.

"And there's a little Italian restaurant right near the campus. We'll have a good time. Just you and me."

I studied him. His suggestion was so unusual I had to think it was connected in some way with what I had discovered.

He said, "Is something the matter?"

Thinking fast, I said, "What about Bobby?"

"You and I are the Sam Spade fans." He smiled and turned away.

"Dad," I said to his back. "Your father died, right?"

"I'm afraid so."

"You sure?"

He swiveled around. "Of course I'm sure. Why would you even ask? Pete, do you have any idea how suspicious you've become?"

"Just curious," I said, retreating while thinking I wouldn't be so suspicious if he'd just tell me the truth.

Next day after school, I went to Mr. Ordson's. Soon as we settled in our chairs—Loki stretched out on the floor—Mr. Ordson said, "You're upset."

"I went to my dad's college and followed him."

"Indeed!"

"Then the FBI followed me."

Hands clasped, the blind man touched his lips with his fingers. "Are you quite sure, Pete?"

"I *told* you. They're trying to find out Dad's secret.

Bobby told the FBI that Dad tells *me* his secrets. So they keep coming after me."

"Why would your brother do such a dreadful thing?"

"So he could go to science camp."

Ordson sighed. "Pete," he said, "isn't this rather like the detective books you read, and those radio shows you listen to?"

"They teach me a lot. That's how I've discovered things. And guess what? I discovered Dad's secret."

"Did you?"

"Dad's been going to a place called the Duffy Nursing Home. His secret is—he's been going to see his father."

"His father!" said Mr. Ordson. "My heavens! Didn't you tell me he died?"

"That's what Dad told me. But I saw him. He's alive."

Ordson sat for a moment in his silent way. Then he said, "Are you . . . positive?"

"Remember what I told you? I saw his picture in Dad's files. And in my Aunt Betty's house. It's him."

"Weren't those photographs taken a long time ago? And didn't you think they were of someone else? Could this just be your imagination taking over?"

"Mr. Ordson, I saw my grandfather in that nursing place. I know it."

"Where has he been all these years?"

"I don't know," I said.

"Did you ask your father?"

"He won't tell me. Keeps saying his father died. He didn't."

"But . . . why would he lie about such a thing?"

"Don't know," I admitted, wishing we could get to the papers.

"Pete," he said, "how did the FBI know you would be at the college so they might follow you?"

"My brother."

"Did you tell Bobby you were going to follow your father?"

"He watched me when I left the house."

"Did you inform him as to where you were going?"

"I don't know how he knew!" I cried. "I just know he did."

When Ordson became quiet, it was obvious to me that he didn't like what I was saying. "I'm right," I said. "I am."

"Very well. Your dad's father is in a nursing home. Do we really believe that's his big secret?"

"Yes."

"But why should it be secret?"

"I don't know!" I yelled, not understanding why Mr. Ordson couldn't get how important my discovery was.

"Pete," said Mr. Ordson, "we live in a time of great mistrust. This is not always a bad thing. People *should* question things. However, in my experience, too much suspicion undermines reason."

I shook my head, only to remember he couldn't see me.

"There's a big difference," he went on, "between suspicion and paranoia."

"What's . . . paranoia?"

"An unreasonable belief that you are being persecuted. For example," Mr. Ordson went on, "I'm willing to guess you've even considered me to be the informer. After all, you told *me* you were going to follow your father. Perhaps *I* told the FBI."

Startled, I stared at him. His blank eyes showed nothing. Neither did his expression. It was as if he had his mask on again.

"*Have* you considered that?" he pushed.

"No," I said. But his question made me realize how much I'd shared with him. Trusted him. How he'd become my only friend. And he was the only one I had told I was going to follow my dad. Maybe he *did* tell the FBI.

He said, "I hope you get my point."

Silence settled around us. Loki looked around, puzzled.

Mr. Ordson must have sensed what I was thinking, because he said, "Now, Pete, you don't really have qualms about me, do you?"

My head was exploding with how stupid I'd been to talk to him. All of a sudden, I didn't want to be there.

Mr. Ordson cleared his throat. "Let's get to the papers."

I was on edge the whole time I read. I kept stealing looks at Mr. Ordson, wishing I could figure out what he was thinking. I *had* told him everything. He knew it all. I wanted to run away.

When we were finished reading, I got to the front door fast. As Mr. Ordson handed me his silver dollar, he said, "Forgive me, Pete. I should not have said that about paranoia. That wasn't fair. Please don't give way to excessive distrust. I fear it is seriously clouding your judgment."

"Mr. Ordson . . ."

"Yes?"

"I can't work for you anymore."

"My goodness, Pete, you mustn't—"

"Got to go," I said, and hurried down the hall.

"Pete," he called after me. "I'll expect you next week. Regular time."

I jumped on the elevator and slapped the buttons with the flat of my hand. The doors thumped shut. The elevator started down, creaking the whole way. My thoughts were tumbling. I should have listened to Dad. Not talked to anyone. No one. If Ordson was an informer, what was I going to do? I'd told him so much.

The moment the elevator jolted to a stop, I stepped out. Behind me, the doors clunked closed. I blinked. It was pitch-black. It was as if I had walked into a trap.

I t took a few seconds for me to understand what had happened: I'd hit the wrong button and landed in the basement.

Fumbling behind me, I located the elevator doorframe. But no call buttons. All I could find was a keyhole. I had to think that one out. Security. If someone stole into the basement area, he couldn't get up into the apartments without a key. To get out, I'd have to search through the dark until I found stairs—there must be stairs somewhere—that would lead to the street.

I stood in place. The cold, clammy basement air irritated my throat. Aside from my rapid breathing, the only noise I heard was the *tick-tick, tick-tick* of a leak, a tinny tattoo touching down as if miles away. All I saw was darkness.

After a few moments, I took some small steps, only to bang into a wall. Frustrated, I started walking in a different direction, but keeping my hands before me.

As I crept forward, I began to see walls. Shadows of a different blackness. But that I could see anything told me light was coming from someplace. I kept going. The light grew, slightly.

I began to see closed doors. I could see labels on them: "Storage 1," "Storage 2." A double set of doors was marked "Main Furnace."

Inching forward, I saw a bend in the walls with some light beyond. I eased around the corner where there was more light. Off to the side was a partly open door. A sign on it read "Telephone Junction Room."

A slice of bright light poked out through the crack between the door and its frame. I was about to go on when I heard the sounds of someone moving around inside the room. Next came the whirr of an electric motor—like a drill.

In a flash, I remembered that detective magazine story "Tapped Out": how the FBI tapped apartment phones from *telephone junction boxes—in basements.* Then that Mario told Ewing—I had been sure it was Ewing—I worked in apartment 4F.

I wanted to get out of there, but I needed to know what was happening in that room. I waited. In moments, a voice came from inside the junction room: "Yeah, just finished. Got it all plugged in. You'll be able to hear everything. I'm leaving now."

That was enough for me. I bolted for that outer door, yanked it open, and dashed out of the building into an alley. The sun was blazing and a green van with the words "Bell Telephone Company" on its side was parked there.

I ran to the main street and kept going. When I got near my own building, on Hicks Street I sat down on the stoop where I used to play stoopball with Kat. I was panting, my heart was galloping, and my thoughts were going just as fast.

As far as I was concerned, I'd heard the sound of the FBI bugging Mr. Ordson's apartment.

On the pavement right in front of me, an army of ants was pouring out of a crack in the sidewalk. There could be thousands of them below, all hidden. Undercover ants.

In the building across the way, someone pulled down a window shade. Was that person hiding something?

Across the street, a new gray Chevy coupe was parked. It had a hood ornament, a rocket, tilted up, as if ready to take off. Maybe Bobby was right: better to escape to the moon. What was that popular Les Paul and Mary Ford song? "How High the Moon." Would the FBI follow me there?

Was Mr. Ordson the informer? Or was he being bugged? Didn't matter. I'd been stupid to talk to him. I wouldn't go back. Couldn't.

I thought of what Mr. Ordson said: that I didn't trust anyone or anything. What was that word he used? *Paranoia.*

I didn't care. As far as I was concerned, Bobby was still the informer.

I tried to think things through. Dad became a Communist about the time he was with Al Depaco. But Depaco told me he knew nothing about that. Was *that* the truth?

I jumped up and went to the phone booth at our corner. I had checked Depaco's phone number so many times I remembered it. Snagging a dime from my pocket, I stepped into the glass-walled booth, dumped my schoolbooks on the ground, dropped the dime into the slot. The dial tone hummed. I spun out TR-5-3218 and waited. The phone rang.

"Hello." Depaco's gravelly voice.

"Hi, Mr. Depaco. This is Pete. Pete Collison. I visited. Remember? Dennis Collison's son."

"Yeah," Depaco barked, with instant anger. "Just so you know, after you left my house the FBI came by. They questioned me."

"They did?"

"You bet they did."

"About . . . what?"

"You. Wanted to know what you were asking me about. Hey, kid, do me a favor. You and your old man. Keep away. I don't want no trouble." He hung up.

I remembered the guy on the subway who I saw both

coming and going. The FBI had followed me to Depaco's house! I wasn't full of paranoia.

Okay: Depaco wasn't the informer.

A little calmer, I was willing to admit that Mr. Ordson wasn't the informer, either. Still, I was sure the FBI was bugging his apartment. The FBI had followed me when I followed Dad. They had talked to Depaco, which meant they must have followed me to his house.

The FBI wanted to talk to me. Ewing kept saying that. Fine. I'd talk to them. Next time they came after me, I'd go after them. They probably wouldn't want anyone to know Bobby was an informer. Fine. I'd make a deal: if the FBI would leave Dad and me alone, I wouldn't tell anyone about Bobby. Of course, I wouldn't tell them about Dad's dad.

Be patient, I told myself. *They're going to come after me again. It'll be the big showdown. Fine.*

On Friday, June 1, I got a coded letter from Kat. When I worked it out, it read:

dear traitor school almost over but not coming
home my parents getting a divorce yuck am going
with my mother to my aunts house for a while
then summer camp then back to this school not
so bad here tried to start a punch ball team but
they said not lady like ha ha so no go miss you
whats up dodgers k

I wrote back, in code.

dear angel sorry about your parents things here
very complicated dont want to put in letter too
many spies and i got paranoya but promise to tell
you all no one to talk to miss you 16 tons plus
3 ounces giants p

Dodgers were in first place. Giants, third.

During the next few days, I kept waiting for the FBI
to show up. They didn't. But then I had a brilliant idea.
Mr. Ewing had invited me to come visit him. Okay, I'd go
to him.

I decided to go on June 5, the day before the anniver-
sary of D-Day, the huge invasion of France during World
War Two. If Dad could be there and survive, I could visit
the FBI office and survive. Then, the following day, I'd
go to that movie with Dad and tell him how I saved him.

I rehearsed what I'd say.

Tuesday, right after school, I ran home, dumped my
books, gulped down a glass of Ovaltine, and walked to
downtown Brooklyn and the Borough Hall building.

*It was in the heart of Brooklyn, but Borough Hall was
as grand and solemn as an ancient Greek temple. It had
wide stone steps, at the top of which stood six huge stone
columns. Ordinary people—none of them in togas—drifted
in and out. In the entrance hall, a guard with a pistol on his
hip sat behind a tall desk. He was probably on the lookout
for Giants fans.*

"Sir," I asked, "can you tell me where I can find the FBI office?"

"What do you want with them, kid?"

I handed him Mr. Ewing's card. "I need to talk to him."

He studied the card. "Something for school?" he asked.

"Sort of," I said, not knowing what else to say.

Pointing with the card, the guard said, "Go down those steps. You'll be in a corridor. Walk toward the end and look for a glass door with 'Federal Bureau of Investigation' on it." He handed the card back to me.

"Thanks."

The hallway was long and deserted, the floor covered with a pattern of small white tiles, like you usually saw in bathrooms. Triple glass light globes hung from the ceiling. Most of the doors had windows of frosted glass, the kind you couldn't see through, with old-fashioned gold lettering:

Office of Parks Management
Department of Waste Licenses

Toward the middle of the hall, I found the door that had

Federal Bureau of Investigation
Brooklyn Office

I stood for a few moments, letting my heart go normal, while I rehearsed what I planned to say. It didn't help that from inside came the sound of fast typing, like a drum rattle. It reminded me of a movie I'd seen. When someone was about to be hanged, they beat a drum that sounded like that.

I pulled the door open.

Pete stepped into a small, well-lit room where a good-looking blonde sat behind a wide desk. On the desk were neat piles of papers, almost as neat as the dame was, along with a typewriter and a phone. Next to the phone was a small American flag on a pedestal, too small for anyone to count the forty-eight stars. A coat tree stood in one corner. The wall behind the blonde had three closed doors and no windows. It didn't seem like the best spot to start searching for secrets, but even dull rooms can hold tons of dynamite. Like the blonde.

The woman who had been typing looked up and gave me a smile that suggested she might do better selling toothpaste.

"Hello. May I help you?"

"I'd like to speak to Mr. Ewing."

"Is he expecting you?"

"He said I could come by if I wanted." When I held out his card I hoped she didn't notice my hand was shaking. She took the card, glanced at it, then me, and said, "Will you tell me your name?"

"Pete Collison."

"Please have a seat, Mr. Collison. I'll see if Mr. Ewing is free."

She went through one of the back doors, her high heels making no sound on the drab office carpet. The door was also noiseless. Pete sat there, thinking about how strange it was to be called "Mr. Collison."

I looked around. There were two pictures on the sky blue wall: One was President Truman. The other face was a man who looked like a bulldog. I didn't know who he was. Up against another wall were a couple of stiff chairs.

There was also a row of wooden file cabinets. If I had X-ray vision, I would have searched the bulging file labeled "Collison."

The secretary reappeared. With her was a smiling Mr. Ewing, the sleeves of his white shirt rolled up. Around his neck hung a loosened gray tie.

"Pete," he called as if we were old friends. "Great to see you." He held out his hand. We shook. It didn't hurt, the way it did the last time.

"Come on back to my office," Ewing said. "Miss Tolin, I don't wish to be disturbed."

"Yes, Mr. Ewing." She said it so nicely I decided she was his girlfriend.

With a touch to my back, Ewing guided me into a pale blue office. There was a wooden desk with a big green blotter, a chair behind it, plus a couple of chairs in front. A folded *Daily News* lay off to one side. Some papers were on the desk. No ashtray. Against one wall were more file cabinets.

"Sit yourself down," Ewing said. He gestured to a chair, then sat behind his desk.

I kept forward on my seat. From the front office, the drumbeat of typing resumed. Every few seconds there was a *ding!* announcing that the secretary had reached the end of a line. I felt as though I had, too.

Still smiling, Ewing leaned forward and clasped his hands. "Nice to see you," he said.

I sat there, unable to get out the words I'd practiced. The rattle of the typewriter rattled me.

"Something important?" he coaxed.

I blurted, "I want you to stop following me."

Though his smile stayed fixed, he unclasped his hands, sat straight. His blue eyes, like headlights, were steady. "What makes you think I'm following you?"

I said, "Black Ford. New York license plate PED459. You followed me from my father's college the other day."

His eyes stayed fixed on me.

"And," I added, bolder now that I had started, "I know you've bugged Mr. Ordson's apartment to hear our conversations."

He didn't move.

"You went to Mr. Depaco's house. Asked him about me."

That time his jaw seemed to tighten.

"I think I know why you're doing it, too."

"Always interested in a good yarn," Ewing said. All business now, he rolled down his sleeves and buttoned them. Adjusted his tie.

"Some informer told you that my father was a Communist when Dad was nineteen. You think my father has more secrets but he won't talk to you. So you're intimidating me to intimidate him."

Mr. Ewing studied me for such a long, silent time that I couldn't keep my eyes up.

"Sounds like you're auditioning for a job with the agency. We could use a good man like you. Bet you listen to that radio show, *This Is Your FBI*."

"Like *The Adventures of Sam Spade, Detective* better."

"Written by a Commie."

"Hammett doesn't even write the shows." When he didn't react, I said, "I just want you to leave my dad alone."

He said, "Pete, my job is to protect the United States of America from its enemies, both domestic and foreign. People who wish to destroy our society and our democratic way of life."

"My dad doesn't want to hurt America."

"Glad to hear it. But there are those who are attempting to do just that, primarily godless Communists."

"I'm not a Communist. I don't like Communists. My dad doesn't either. He's a socialist."

"No difference."

"Is!"

"Pete, we believe your father has information that would help us do our job."

"That what the informer told you?"

When he said nothing, I considered telling him I knew

the informer was Bobby, but I held back, waiting to make my deal. "If you leave my dad alone . . . I won't reveal the name of your informer."

He actually seemed to consider it. "Look, Pete, if your dad is a good, patriotic American—as you claim—who has broken no laws, he has absolutely nothing to worry about. Neither do you."

I said, "Then stop following me."

He was quiet for a while. "You have a reputation for knowing family secrets."

"My brother tell you that?"

"You're a lot closer to your dad than he is."

"How do you know?"

The smile returned, tighter this time. "It's my job to know things."

"I bet you told—Mr. Donavan—that my dad was a Communist. Want to know what happened after that? Donavan made everyone in my class hate me. They called me 'Commie.' Won't talk to me. Won't even let me play punchball. My best friend was sent away."

Ewing snorted. "We're fighting a war against Reds and you can't play punchball, huh? The Commies might drop an A-bomb on us but your best friend went away. Poor Pete."

"Leave me alone!" I shouted. The typing in the other room stopped. Was Miss Tolin listening to the conversation?

Ewing continued to gaze at me. Then he stood, went to one of the file cabinets, and opened it. His fingers ran along the tabs. He pulled out a file, sat down, and opened it. "Your grandfather, Thomas Collison," he said, reading, "went to the Soviet Union in 1934 under a contract with the Amtorg Trading Corporation. Worked at the Ford factory the Soviets rebuilt."

So Dad's father did go to Russia.

Ewing, still looking at the file, went on. "Like most Americans who went to Soviet Russia, your grandfather was probably arrested and sent to a Siberian labor camp, where he worked like a slave, died, or was forced into the Red Army."

In my head I said, *He doesn't know my grandfather is alive.*

Ewing closed the folder and flipped it to one side. "Let me tell you, Pete, if we let the Commies take over, that's exactly how people will be treated here."

And he doesn't know my grandfather has come back to America.

"He just wanted to find work," I mumbled.

Ewing clasped his hands. "Maybe." Then he said, "The name Nelson Kasper mean anything to you?"

I shook my head.

"Listen, Pete," said Ewing. "I like you. You're a good kid. Smart. It took guts to come here. If you really want to help your father, tell him to cooperate with the U.S. government."

"How?"

"By helping us find your grandfather."

"He just wanted work," I said again.

Ewing said, "Maybe your grandfather wasn't killed. Maybe he became a Commie spy."

I had never thought of that. It shook me. It took me a moment to recover. "What . . . what if my dad doesn't help you?"

"Not good. But if *you* can tell us things, I promise we won't trouble him. Maybe he can hang on to his job."

"Tell you what?" I whispered.

"Things about your father. Your grandfather. Did you know your father was a Communist before I told you? Did you know your grandfather went to the Soviet Union?"

I shook my head.

"Listen, Pete, my job is to see what's going on in our country. I intend to do exactly that."

"Did you bug Mr. Ordson's apartment?"

Ewing said, "You could tell us what your dad talks about—when he talks politics. Does he have friends who are Commies? And who does he visit at the Duffy Nursing Home?"

"You're asking me to spy on my dad."

He leaned forward. Without the trace of a smile on his face, he said, "Hey, Pete, isn't that exactly what you've been doing?"

If he had thrown a brick at my head, it couldn't have hurt more.

He must have guessed my reaction. He said, "I think we'd work well together. Still rooting for the Giants?"

"Yeah."

He reached for his newspaper and turned over a few pages. "Says here the Giants are in fifth place behind the Dodgers. Twelve games out of first place. Want some advice, Pete?"

"I guess."

"Pick winners." He tossed the paper aside. "Your brother has."

His words jolted me back to life. "What's that mean?"

"Bobby wants to go to the moon, right? Only one way he can get there. The U.S. government. Maybe I offered a recommendation for something he wanted to do in return for a little help."

I jumped up. Far as I was concerned, Ewing just confirmed that Bobby was the informer. I said, "I'm going to tell my family who the informer is."

For once, I landed a punch. He sat back. "Pete, it would be a serious mistake to interfere with what we do."

"I'm telling!" I shouted, and bolted from the room. I wasn't so much leaving as escaping.

Behind me, I heard Ewing shout: "Don't be a loser, Pete."

I ran out of the building and didn't slow down until I was on the street. The farther I walked, the more I began to think about what I had just learned, facts as sharp as needles.

First: Ewing told me Dad's father *had* gone to the Soviet Union.

Second: He didn't know he had come back and that he was in the nursing home.

Third: Maybe my grandfather was a Soviet spy.

Fourth: Ewing all but admitted Bobby was the informer.

But . . . maybe Bobby was doing a good thing by being an informer. Protecting the U.S. from spies. Turning Dad in, the way Sam Spade turned in the woman he loved.

Then I realized something: Ewing had asked me if I knew a Nelson Kasper. It was one of the names on the photo Dad had.

Who was he?

I was supposed to go with Dad to see that Sam Spade movie tomorrow. We'd be alone and out of the house. It was time to tell him everything I had discovered. Get answers. Time to throw my dynamite stick of truth.

N ext day, I spent all of school—four hundred and
fifty minutes—watching the hands on the classroom
clock. They moved as if someone had stuck bubble gum into
the works. We also had a bomb drill. I told myself it was
good practice for the explosion I was going to drop on Dad.

As the day wore on, I felt my insides being wound
tighter and tighter. Was I really going to tell Dad about
Bobby and what I had found about his dad? Or that the
FBI thought my grandfather was a spy?

Yes.

After school, I made my way to Dad's college office. It was stuffed with American history books. On the
walls were pictures of George Washington and Abraham

Lincoln. Between them was a realistic copy of the Declaration of Independence. When I walked in, Dad was sitting behind his messy desk, reading.

Soon as I appeared, he put his book down, and flipped an orange and black New York Giants sweatshirt at me. "Like it?" he said, grinning.

"Yeah. Nice."

"Too bad they aren't doing well. Brooklyn is first. Where are the Giants?"

As I pulled the sweatshirt over my head, I said, "Fourth."

"Oh, well. Wait till next year."

I remembered my bet with Kat.

"You're going to love this movie, Pete," he said as we walked toward the college theater. "It won two Academy Awards and is on lots of 'Best Ever' movie lists. Humphrey Bogart is great as Sam Spade."

The theater was half full, mostly with students. A few waved to Dad as we found seats. A girl rushed up and said to him, "Professor Collison, is this your son?"

"Sure is."

"He looks like you. Your father is the chili," she said to me and ran off.

"What's 'chili' mean?"

He laughed. "I think she means I'm okay."

What would they think when they learned he was hiding a Soviet spy?

I had read *The Maltese Falcon* a bunch of times, so I knew the story: a gang was after an ancient jeweled bird.

Everybody lies, cheats, double-crosses, and kills one another to get it. You're not supposed to know who's good or bad—except for Sam Spade, of course. Turns out the worst crook is the lady he loves. But he turns her over to the police the way I imagined myself turning in Bobby.

Right then I knew I could never do it.

After we walked to the restaurant, I said, "The part I never get is Spade really loved that woman, right?"

"Right. Brigid O'Shaughnessy."

"But he handed her over to the cops."

"Because she killed his partner. He has to be loyal to what he believes."

"You think he did right?" I asked.

He said, "Pal, if you ever look up the word *right* in a dictionary, you'll find it's one of the oldest words in the English language. Even so, people have never stopped arguing about what it means. I suspect they always will."

The restaurant was called Little Italy. Inside, a dozen people sat at round tables covered with red-and-white checkered tablecloths. On each table were a glass ashtray and an empty wine bottle wrapped in straw. A lit candle stuck out the top, dripping red wax. From somewhere unseen, accordion music oozed like sweet syrup. Cigarette smoke layered the air like a zebra's ghost.

Dad pointed to the glossy pictures on the wall. "The Leaning Tower of Pisa. The Roman Colosseum. Saint Peter's. All in Italy. Someday we should go."

A waitress came over. My father ordered. "A couple of Cokes and a pizza with everything."

"What's . . . pizza?" I asked.

"It's the new hit. You'll love it." Dad was having a good time. His face was so relaxed I hated to ruin it. But I decided this was the best time to talk.

I hunched over the table. "Dad, got some huge things to tell you."

"Shoot."

I took a deep breath and said, "I went to the FBI office."

Dad's mouth fell open. "You did *what?*" His voice was a choked whisper.

I said, "I spoke to that FBI agent, Mr. Ewing. The one who came to our house."

He stared at me with disbelieving eyes. "Why?" he said. The word came at me like a sharp arrow.

"For you," I said.

"Is this a joke?"

"No. I . . . I really went."

Dad patted his pocket, looking for cigarettes. Not finding any, he leaned forward. All the fun had fled from his face. Anger replaced it. In a hard voice he said, "Talk. But keep it down."

Struggling to speak, I said, "I wanted . . . the FBI to leave you—and me—alone. Stop, you know, trying to intimidate me. I . . . I told Ewing if he stopped I wouldn't tell anyone who the informer is."

"I don't know what you are talking about."

"The informer, Dad. You know. The one who told . . . them you were a"—I lowered my voice even more—"a Communist."

"Good Lord."

The waitress came. She brought our Cokes, put them down, and went off. The Cokes' bouncing bubbles looked like jitterbuggers. I couldn't move to take a sip.

"Go on," said Dad. "The informer . . ."

"See, I figured out who he is."

"Who?"

I was about to throw my Sam Spade explosion. I couldn't.

"Pete, you need to tell me," Dad pushed. "Who is the informer?"

"Bobby."

A blockbuster bomb all right. He turned pale. His bad arm jerked as if he'd been shot again, and he looked at me as if he had never seen me before.

I shrank down in my chair.

"*Bobby?*" he gasped.

I gave a nod that was mostly a shiver. The silence that followed smothered us.

Dad rubbed his mustache. "I think," he said after a few moments, "you'd better explain."

Struggling, I said, "Remember when you and I talked, and you told me you were a . . . you know . . ."

"Okay."

"Bobby was in the hallway, listening."

"That's not the end of the world. Besides, you told me that the agent who talked to you . . . about me . . . spoke *before* you and I had our conversation. So what could Bobby tell them that they didn't already know?"

I wanted to say, "About your father," but it was too hard to say. All I said was, "Something else. Your secret."

Dad just sat there for a moment, eyes hard on me. Then he said, "Pete, tell me again what Mr. Ewing said to you that day he came to the apartment."

"He asked me about your father. What happened to him. Wanted to know about your family. Then, when I went to see him, he told me your father went to the Soviet Union—just like you told me. I'm pretty sure Bobby was listening and told him."

The waitress delivered the pizza. It was a wheel of flat bread on a big tin platter. The bread had this tomato sauce on it along with cheese and meat bits. It looked like someone's throw-up. I lost my appetite.

"Pete," said Dad in a low, urgent voice, "I *never* told you my father went to the Soviet Union because I've never told *anyone*. What I said—to you—was that he was *thinking* about going."

"The FBI guy told me he . . . went," I said, feebly. "So, somebody must have known and . . . told him."

"If they had that information it could have come from a thousand different sources. Our government. The Soviet government. I have no idea. And I don't care," he added fiercely.

I felt the way I did when Dad beat me in checkers after three moves: dumb.

Dad wasn't done. "Pete, why would you even *think* Bobby would do such a thing?"

I said, "He wanted to get into that space camp."

"How are they connected?"

"Ewing told me they were." I repeated what he told me.

Dad said, "I refuse to believe it. Get a kid to spy on his father? Not even *they* would stoop that low. Did you tell your brother this?"

I shook my head.

"Good." Dad's tension eased. "*Don't!* Pete, you've acted like some junior G-man. A simpleminded Sam Spade."

I slumped in my seat. I couldn't even look at Dad.

"Pal, the thing about detectives is that like historians, they need to be suspicious. Of people. Of what people say. What they don't say. Of clues. Both try to get the truth, not what they *want* the truth to be, but what *is* true. And guess what? Sometimes it's hard to know the difference. I think that's the mistake you made here, Pete."

I kept my head down.

"Know why detectives are called gumshoes?"

I shook my head.

"The name comes from gum-rubber soles on shoes. They're quiet. In other words, a detective is someone who walks softly. You might give it a try."

I stared at the table.

"You don't like Bobby, do you?"

"He's always telling me how dumb I am."

"You're not dumb. Like most everybody—me included—you can do dumb things. And brothers—teenage brothers—that's a whole different story. That's no reason to accuse Bobby, is it?"

I shook my head.

"So we agree? No more about him. Not to me. Not to him. Promise?"

"Promise," I said.

We were quiet for a moment while he studied me with worried eyes. "Is that it, Pete? If there's more I suppose I'd better hear."

If there had been a hole nearby, I'd have crawled in.

"Come on, Pal. It can't be worse than what you've already said."

But I knew it was.

34

Dad sat there, waiting. I had to force myself to look at him. "The other reason I went to the FBI was . . . I wanted them to stop following me."

"Were they?"

"Told you: They think you have some secret and that you told me. So they keep coming after me. That day I was suspended from school, Mr. Ewing tried to talk to me."

"Where?"

"Home."

"Pete! That's serious. How come you never told us?"

"I didn't talk to him. He came to the door but I didn't let him in."

Dad thought for a moment, and then said, "How did he know you were there and not in school?"

"I thought . . . Bobby told him."

"Pete—"

"I know. But there's something else."

"Let's hear it." Dad looked exhausted, but I made myself go on. "I went to visit your old friend, Al Depaco."

Dad had been sipping his Coke, but hearing the name, he put it down so quickly it sloshed over. "Al Depaco? How do you even know about him? Did you actually speak to him?"

I nodded. "And the thing is, afterwards, the FBI visited him and warned him to keep away from me. And I think I caught the FBI bugging Mr. Ordson's phone. See, they keep hoping to get your secret. From me."

Dad said nothing but he kept his eyes—now full of puzzlement—fixed on me. "What secret?" he said.

I said, "I didn't know it before. But I . . . do now."

"What in the world are you talking about?"

I couldn't speak.

"Keep talking," said Dad.

"The other day I wanted to see where you were going on Wednesdays. So . . . I followed you."

"You did *what?*"

"Followed you. To that . . . Duffy Nursing Home. And . . . the FBI followed me there."

"Good Lord. Did they see me go in?"

"Maybe."

Beads of sweat stood out on his head. His eyes became sad, his mustache more ragged, his mouth tight, and there were lines on his face. It was as if what I'd said made him older. It was awful to see. Scary.

"Pete, what else did you do?"

"I went in and saw your . . . secret. Your dad. My grandfather. That's your secret."

Dad rubbed his face and closed his eyes. He swallowed. Shook his head. "Pete," he said in a hoarse whisper, leaning toward me. "I told you again and again: My father died a long time ago."

"Dad," I pleaded in the same low voice, "when I went to Ewing, he told me your father went to the Soviet Union. But they don't know your father is alive and back in America. Just think he might be. And they think he might be a spy. I won't tell anyone, I promise."

Dad sat there looking baffled. When he didn't speak, I said, "Is he . . . a spy?"

"Pete," Dad said, "my father is *not* alive."

"Then who is—"

"Didn't I tell you not to get involved in this?"

The man and woman at the nearest table looked over to us.

"How do you know all this stuff?" Dad asked in an angry whisper. "Depaco. My father. Good God! You're no different than the FBI!"

Guilt flooded me. That was what Ewing had said. If

you can hate yourself, I did then. All the same, I admit, I still wanted to know who Dad had been visiting and why it was a secret.

Dad sat there looking like a tire that had lost its air. Finally, he said, "You going to eat anything?"

"No."

He stood up. "Let's get out of here."

He paid the bill and we started walking. I had to work at keeping up with him. We didn't talk.

Abruptly Dad stopped and said, "Just so you know: The day after you followed me to the nursing home they called me and said someone was asking about me, wondering who I was visiting. The Home won't give out that kind of information without first checking."

"Who called?" I said.

"I don't know. Probably your friend, Ewing."

"He's not my friend," I protested. When he continued to stand there I said, "Did he find your father?"

"Pete, my father is not there. He's dead!"

"Then . . . who was that man?"

Dad just stood there for a moment, as if unable to find himself. When he finally spoke, he spoke more to the air than to me. "My brother," he said.

"Frank?"

"How do you . . . No, not here." Looking wretched, Dad rubbed his bad arm. "We need to get home," he said. We headed toward the subway in silence, me too stunned to ask more questions.

When we came to a drugstore, he said, "Stay here." He went inside and came back with a pack of cigarettes. We walked on, me checking his face for clues. There were none.

We reached the subway steps. Instead of going down, Dad stopped. He leaned back against the stair rail for support, took out a cigarette, and lit it in his awkward way. The lit match gave his face a ruddy glow before the flame faded to black. Like a movie.

Something Kat had said came into my mind. "What'll happen when you find out those things?" I didn't know the answer, but I had the feeling I was about to find out.

O kay," Dad began, his voice low, full of pain. "I was nineteen," he said. "My father had gone, I didn't know where. As it turned out, only Frank knew—he was really close to my dad—but Frank wasn't saying.

"The family was broke. Not much food. Not much of anything. My mother was angry. Bitter. She told me I had to drop out of school and earn money. Uncle Chris, who sort of took over my father's role, was being rough on me.

"I left home for two reasons: I had to get away from Uncle Chris and I wanted to stay in school. Those days, lots of kids were leaving their homes. Al Depaco and I decided to go together.

"Then I learned—from Frank—that my father was still

in the city and was about to go to Soviet Russia. Frank, who was sixteen at the time, wanted to go with him.

"I was Frank's big brother. He always listened to me. Like Bobby, I was a cocky know-it-all. Hey, maybe Frank would have a better life there. Life was rough here. I urged Frank to go. He went.

"Frank was my mother's favorite. Her baby. If she could have grabbed the moon, she would have given it to him. And maybe my father encouraged Frank to go with him to get at her.

"I didn't know that my father hadn't told my mother what he was doing. Nor did Frank. Turns out, I was the only one who knew where they were going.

"Loyal to my brother, I said nothing to my mother. Having secrets makes kids feel independent. It can also make things worse.

"I assumed they'd be back. But by the time I realized Frank wasn't coming back, I was afraid to say anything. Anyway, I had left home, too. Then, when Al told me Uncle Chris had tracked me down, I took off on my own. As far as I was concerned, I had no family to go back to. Besides, not telling my mother what I knew about Frank and my father made me feel guilty. Feeling guilty is like quicksand. The more you wiggle to get out, the deeper you sink.

"I sank.

"After the war, America was full of optimism. By then I'd married, had you kids, and wanted to start fresh. I got back together with my family. Your grandma never mentioned Frank. Nor did I. I felt too guilty. Truth is, I'm ashamed of how I acted."

"Sorry," I whispered, only to have what Kat said, "Sorry is a sorry word," come into my head. "How come nobody talks about Frank?" I asked.

"Nobody—except me—knew where he went. When years went by without hearing from him, we all assumed he died." Dad took a deep drag on his cigarette. "Being silent is a kind of death."

I said, "What happened to him?"

"In Soviet Russia? At the start, things worked. My father had a decent job. Frank went to school. Then the Soviets took away the Americans' passports. Said they were now Soviet citizens. Frank wanted to come home. The Communists wouldn't let him. Frank went to our embassy. The U.S. asked for proof he was an American. He had none.

"It wasn't long before he and my father were sent to ghastly prison labor camps. My father died there.

"When the war came, Frank was given a choice: stay in that prison camp, or join the Red Army.

"He joined. Fought against the Nazis. He and I were fighting the same war, same enemy, from different sides.

"At the end of the war, when the Russian and American armies linked up in Germany, there was lots of mingling between the armies. Frank came upon the body of a dead American soldier. His tags read Nelson Kasper. Frank got out of his Soviet uniform, into Kasper's, crossed to the

American lines. Just like that. He was an American. He came home as Nelson Kasper.

"He started life again in the state of Washington. Little town called Blaine right on the Canadian border. In case he had to run away.

"Frank was free, but he lived in fear that he'd be discovered and sent back to the Soviet Union. If he was, he'd be killed. At the same time, he couldn't tell our government what he'd done. He had left America. Been made—albeit against his will—a Russian citizen. Worst of all, he had impersonated a dead U.S. soldier."

"How do you know all this?" I asked.

"A few months ago Frank called me. Talk about shock. I didn't believe it was him at first. He asked me to call him. BLaine 2573. A rural phone number. When I called, Frank told me his story. And . . ." Dad trailed off.

"And what?"

"He was worn out. Like an old man. Sick. Dying. That's why he wanted to get in touch with me. To tell me what happened while he had the chance. I brought him to New York. Got him into that nursing home."

"He looks a lot older than you."

"He's had a ghastly life. He won't live long."

"He a Commie?"

"Pete," Dad said, "how can you even ask?"

"You going to tell Grandma about Frank? Your family?"

Dad shook his head.

"Why not?"

"Frank doesn't want me to. It's been too many years. He just wants to die in peace on clean sheets. I respect that."

Dad became quiet, just stood there, smoking his cigarette. His eyes had a faraway look. I was sure his mind was with his brother.

"Dad," I said, "is Frank's life your fault?"

"I urged him to go, didn't I? Pete, I want you to promise, *promise* you'll stay out of this from now on."

"Can I ask one question?"

"Do you have to?"

"What would the FBI do if they got to your brother?"

"Probably arrest him. Put him in jail. Deport him to Soviet Russia, where I suppose he'd go into another jail. Dying in jail is no way to end your life."

"Ewing never said anything about your having a brother."

"Good. Whoever called the Duffy Home asked if I was visiting Thomas Collison, my father. I registered my brother under his new name, Nelson Kasper, so I think he's safe. Your ma knows the name. Now you. It's just the three of us. No one else."

But Bobby must have seen the name in Dad's file folder. Ewing knew it, too. As far as I was concerned, it had to be Bobby who had given him the name.

"Let's go home," said Dad. He led the way down to the subway platform.

We got on the train. I sat there thinking about Dad's

brother. Being in Soviet Russia. Escaping. Hiding in America by pretending to be someone else.

As the train roared along, Dad bent over and said, "Since we're sharing secrets, you might as well know: I've been told more about my summer date with that committee. They've told me what they are going to ask."

"Do they know about your father and brother?"

"Not sure. I do know they'll ask me if I am a Communist. If I ever was a Communist. I don't believe they have the right to ask those questions, but I'm willing to talk about myself. The trouble is, they've told me they want me to name other people I knew who were Communists. Or maybe it's really about my father or Frank."

"What are you going to say?"

Dad gave me a serious look. "My father is gone. I won't talk about my brother. Other people can speak for themselves. It's not my place to tell the government what people think. I believe in the First Amendment. Freedom of speech. Like Sam Spade, you've got to be loyal to what you believe."

"That why you wanted me to see the movie?"

"Maybe."

"You going to jail?"

"I might."

"Would it be awful?"

"Probably." Then he added, "Frank survived much worse."

I sat there, plain old scared.

The subway roared on, swaying, stopping, starting, people getting off and on. They didn't look at one another.

Dad leaned over. "Pete, do you still remember the key part of the Declaration of Independence?"

I nodded. "'We hold these truths to be self-evident, that all men are created equal, that they are endowed by their Creator with certain unalienable rights, that among these are life, liberty and the pursuit of happiness.'"

Dad said: "That's the best, simplest, most beautiful sentence about liberty. But . . ."

"What?"

"Thomas Jefferson, the man who wrote that—about liberty—owned slaves. Owned *people*. Pete, nothing is simple. Know that and you know half the world's wisdom."

Soon as we got home, I went to my room and lay on my bed, face in a pillow. I felt awful. Working to make things better for my father, I'd actually made things worse by leading the FBI to that nursing place. Same time, I still thought I was right about Bobby. He'd been in Dad's files. I was sure he'd seen Dad's brother's new name. It had to be him who had given that name "Nelson Kasper" to the FBI.

Ma came into my room. Before she said anything, I rolled away from her and said, "Don't want to talk."

She left me alone.

When Bobby came in, he said, "What's going on? Giants lose another one? You actually going to wear that sweatshirt around here?"

It took effort to keep my mouth shut.

In the radio room, with all of us there, Dad told Bobby what he already told me, his summons to the committee.

Bobby said, "You going to lose your job?"

"I'm not sure. It'll be during the summer. Maybe no one will notice." His thin smile told me he didn't really believe it.

Ma said, "I'll still have my job. Our apartment is rent controlled."

Dad said, "You should also know I might be sent to jail."

"Why?" said Bobby.

Keeping my eyes on him, I said, "He won't be an informer."

No one said anything. I watched Bobby and tried to read his face. Nothing. It made me remember what Dad had said: "Being silent is a kind of death."

The death of our family.

Then I remembered my promise to Dad. *It can't be Bobby,* I told myself. *Stop thinking it's Bobby. It's NOT Bobby!*

Then who?

36

A week later, the following Thursday, I left school at three o'clock as usual. After all that had happened, suspicion had become my middle name. I was watchful, paying attention to things around me. That's why I noticed the gray Chevy, the one with the rocket on its hood.

As soon as I saw that rocket ornament, I remembered the car I'd seen near our apartment building a few weeks ago. Now the car was behind me, coming slowly down the street, not passing me, which it could have done easily.

I'd told Ewing I knew about his Ford. That was stupid. He'd changed cars.

I kept going. Once, twice, I looked over my shoulder. The Chevy was creeping along, right behind me. I stopped.

It stopped. I walked faster. The car went faster. It was obvious the driver wanted me to know he was stalking me. It was like that time Ewing first followed me home from school in early April.

I reached a corner, made a sudden right turn, and started to run. From behind came the squeal of tires. I looked back. The Chevy was coming.

Mid-block, I ran across the street and sped round another corner. The car roared and shot past me, too fast for me to see who was driving. If he wanted to terrify me, he succeeded.

I doubled back, running hard. The gray car made a U-turn and kept following me. When I reached the end of the block, I realized I was close to Mr. Ordson's apartment. It was the closest, safest place. I ran for it.

The door was locked and Mario wasn't there to open it. I pushed Mr. Ordson's call button. When an answer didn't come, I pushed it again and again, continually looking back over my shoulder to check the street. I didn't see anyone coming, not yet.

At last, a voice from the squawk box said, "Who is it, please?"

"Mr. Ordson. It's me, Pete. I need to come in."

The lock buzzed. I threw my weight against the door and plunged inside. I slammed the door shut behind me, making sure the lock clicked. Then I headed for the elevator, only to see the numbers over the elevator telling me it was on the fourth floor, Ordson's floor.

I headed for the steps. Halfway to the first level, I came upon Mario mopping the steps.

"Hi, Pete. Sorry. You better take the elevator. Or the other steps. These are slippery."

I spun round and started down, halting before entering the lobby again to make sure no one was coming in through the front doors. As I was looking, someone came rushing down the other steps, crossed the lobby, and ran out the front door.

It was Ewing.

Astonished, I rushed down the rest of the steps into the lobby and peered out the front doors. I didn't see Ewing or the Chevy. Even so, I was afraid to go out to the street.

Behind me, the elevator returned to the lobby. Its door cranked open. I hesitated. But if Ewing had been with Mr. Ordson, I needed to find out.

After checking to make sure no one was hiding in the elevator, I headed up. On the fourth floor, my hand shaking, I pushed the doorbell button on Mr. Ordson's door.

"Who is it?"

"It's me, Mr. Ordson, Pete."

The door opened. Loki stuck out his nose and wagged his tail. Mr. Ordson stood there. "Pete," he said. "I am so glad you came. You'll never believe who was just here."

I said, "The FBI."

"Exactly. That same Agent Ewing about whom you told me. He was actually asking if you had said anything to me about your father. When you buzzed, I told this Mr. Ewing it was you, hoping it would embarrass him. He left immediately. Did you see him?"

"Yeah."

"As for his questions, of course I refused to answer. The gall. Coming here and inquiring about you. I thought we fought wars to stop that kind of thing. Please, Pete, come in. We need to talk."

"I don't want to."

"For heaven's sake, Pete, you can trust me. Though I can tell you're very agitated. Has something happened?"

"Mr. Ordson," I said, "the last time I was here, did someone come to fix your phone?"

"What an odd question. Let me think. That was . . . Actually, yes, someone did come. Apparently, there was a telephone problem in the apartment below. A man came to see if there were crossed wires in my place."

"Did you know him?"

"No, Mario handled it. Told me about it afterwards."

"Mr. Ordson, I think it was the FBI bugging your apartment."

"Pete, I refuse to believe that."

I told Ordson what I'd seen and heard in his basement.

He said, "Pete, you can't be sure. This is an old building. Things are always breaking down."

I told him what just happened. About the gray car chasing me.

He said, "Are you certain that car was the FBI? Since

Ewing was here, he couldn't very well have been driving the car, could he?"

"Mr. Ordson, did you tell Ewing any of the stuff I told you?"

"Absolutely not. Now please step in, Pete, and we can discuss all this."

"Mr. Ordson, I can't talk to you anymore."

"But Pete—"

"I can't."

"Well, in your present state I must honor that. Nonetheless I will insist that Loki and I walk you home."

Which is what happened. A blind man and his Seeing Eye dog led me home.

When we reached the doorway to my apartment, Mr. Ordson said, "Pete, I urge you to discuss this with your parents. And please, come back at your regular time. I hope we're still friends."

"Thanks," I said.

That night Mr. Ordson called me on the telephone.

"Pete," he said, "I wanted to tell you I spoke to Mario about that repairman. I asked him if anything struck him as unusual. About the man's visit."

"What did he say?"

"The telephone company simply showed up and said they needed to do some repairs. Mario let them. As far as he was concerned it was perfectly legitimate."

I said, "But you can't be sure, can you? They're probably listening right now."

"Everything is not connected, Pete."

"It is," I said.

"Pete," he said, "do come back. We can talk about it."

"I can't," I said, and hung up.

I didn't tell my parents what happened. Why should I? I knew what was going on. I'd told the FBI I knew who the informer was. Had threatened to tell people. Now they were threatening *me* again but I wouldn't tell. I couldn't. The joke—if you wanted to call it that—was that I had made myself accept that it was not Bobby.

Still, there was nagging in my head. Wasn't I—like Sam Spade—supposed, no matter *what,* to find the truth?

N ext day I got a code letter from Kat:

dear traitor school almost over some girls are
nice teachers okay what are you doing for summer will you go back to ps ten my father came
here and told me it was my mothers fault they
wont stay married next week my mother came
and told me it was my fathers fault they wont
stay married this week no one came so maybe it
is my fault wish i had your family but that would
mean i would have to marry you and you are a
giants fan too bad k

I wrote back, in code:

```
dear angel things are so mixed up my family not
good wish i could talk to you maybe i will find a
way to visit you somewhere in the world then i
could tell you everything because it would take
so long to write i think i will be mostly here all
summer will you i still believe in the giants and
miss you
p
```

On June 18, Brooklyn was still in first place. The Giants were in second, six games behind.

A few days later, a week before summer vacation began, I walked out of school and stood on the top step. As I'd come to do, I looked around for the Ford or Chevy. I didn't see either of them. Even so, I kept checking as I walked home. It was when I got home that I saw the FBI Ford parked in front of my house.

My heart squeezed.

Ewing was sitting behind the wheel. When he saw me, he jumped out of the car.

I froze.

"Hey, Pete," Ewing called. "I was just coming to talk to you." He drew closer, holding out his hand.

I didn't move but I said, "I told you I knew who the informer was. I don't know. So just leave my father alone. Same for Mr. Ordson. I'm sorry for interfering. Just leave me alone, please!" I was yelling now. "I don't know anything!"

"Come on, Pete, talk to me. I'm your friend!"

I ran past him and into our building. Once in our apartment I slammed the door, locked it, and made sure the door chain was on. Then I ran to the front window and looked down at the street and the Ford. The doorbell began to ring. It rang again. I didn't answer. There were a few minutes of silence, and then the phone began to ring. I saw Ewing in the corner phone booth. He was calling me. I didn't answer. After a while, he gave up.

For the rest of the afternoon, I lay on my bed, a pillow over my head. Long after Ewing was gone, I kept hearing his call, "I'm your friend!" I felt so cold.

Next day at school, when the three o'clock bell rang, I went out the main school doors and scanned the street. The gray Chevy was parked at the end of the block, facing me. I spun round and went back to my classroom.

Mr. Donavan was at his desk, an open ledger in front of him. He was writing. When I came in, he looked up.

"Yes, Pete?"

"I forgot something," I said. What I really wanted to do was look out the window and see if that car had stayed there.

Donavan turned back to his work.

I went to my desk, found a textbook, and pulled it out. My desk was right next to the window, so I could steal a look down to the street. The gray Chevy hadn't budged. Heart pounding, I headed for the door.

Donavan looked up. "Pete," he called.

I stopped.

"Were you intending to return to this school next year?"

That took me by surprise. "I guess."

"You and your parents might reconsider it."

"Why?"

"The other day I was called to the office. A friend of mine from the FBI was there asking about you. He wanted to know if you lied a lot. I told him I had no experience with you lying, but in class you repeated your father's Communist propaganda."

I said, "Is that what you told Ewing?"

His face showed surprise. "Do you know him?"

"He's a friend of mine," I said. "And he's sitting right outside, waiting for me."

"He is?" He frowned.

It wasn't hatred I felt for Donavan, it was disgust. "You know what," I blurted out, "you're a bully. I'm going to tell Ewing you lie about me."

His face got all red.

I walked out.

By the time I got to the street, the Chevy was gone. I sat on the school steps and stared at the spot where it had been. I had to admit that I hadn't actually seen Ewing in that car. He had always been in the black Ford. And that time the Chevy had come after me, as Mr. Ordson said,

Ewing was with him. So the person driving the Chevy couldn't have been Ewing. And Bobby didn't drive. I decided it was another FBI agent.

On the last day of school—Friday, June 22—we stood in line to hand in our textbooks. When I gave mine to Mr. Donavan, I said, "I'll be back next year."

He barely glanced at me. Just took the book and flipped through the pages, looking for doodles. Wordlessly, he placed it on a pile with other books. Then he handed me my yellow report card.

I stepped into the hall and opened the card. Donavan had given me a D in everything. But at the bottom, he had written

Promoted to Eighth Grade.

As far as I was concerned, those D grades were like Dad's Purple Heart. I had survived.

Out on the street, kids were milling around, shouting, fooling, saying good-bye, making plans about getting together, telling each other their summer hopes. I walked through them as invisible as ever. Didn't speak to anyone. No one spoke to me.

I made a quick trip to Ritman's and bought an old *Detective Magazine*. My walk home up Hicks Street felt like a walk to nowhere. I had no idea what I was going to do that summer. Ma had most of the summer off. Would

Bobby be going to his camp or would Ewing stop him? Then there was Dad's committee hearing. If he lost his job, if he was sent to jail, I didn't know what would happen.

I got home and checked the lobby table for mail, hoping I'd find a letter from Kat. Was her school over? Had she come home? Where was she?

There was one letter for Ma, one for Bobby. Bobby's letter was from the National Advisory Committee for Aeronautics, the people running his summer rocket camp. I put Ma's letter on the kitchen table, dropped Bobby's on his bed.

In the kitchen, I called Kat's number. A voice said, "We are sorry, but this number has been disconnected."

Sorry is a sorry word. Wondering if I would ever see her again, all I could feel was sadness.

I drank some chocolate milk, ate a Twinkie, and then went into the radio room and started reading my new magazine.

Ma was the first to get home. Big smile. "How was your last day at school?"

"I got promoted to eighth grade."

"Congratulations! One more year and it's high school."

Bobby came home and passed through the room without saying anything to me. Moments later I heard him give an angry yelp.

I jumped up and went over to his side. Face full of fury, Bobby was standing there, holding a piece of paper in his hand. He began to swear. Ma rushed in.

"What is it?" she said.

"They dropped me from summer rocket camp!" screamed Bobby.

"Why?"

He shook the paper at her. "Says I have"—he read from the letter—"a close and continued association with my father, Dennis Collison, who is currently under suspicion for subversive activities by federal authorities."

"Oh, Bobby," said Ma. "That's awful. I'm so sorry."

"It ruins everything," Bobby cried. "My whole life." He swore purple again.

I said nothing.

Dinner that night was just me, Ma, and Dad. Bobby refused to come. There was very little talk. To Dad I said, "I got promoted to eighth grade."

"I'm proud of you," said Dad.

Later, I was reading on my bed when I heard Bobby move around on his side of the room. I called out, "Sorry about your camp."

"What do you care?" he shot back.

"Said I'm sorry."

"Liar," he said. "It's your fault."

I sat up. "What are you talking about?"

"They promised me. But you had to muck it up."

"Who promised what?"

"That I'd get into the camp. Then you went to the FBI and screwed it up."

I jumped off my bed and stood by the partition. Bobby

was at his desk, bent over, head resting in his arms. I said, "How do you know I went to the FBI?"

He gave no answer.

"What did the FBI promise you?"

"Think I'm going to tell an idiot like you?"

"You just said that because I went to the FBI they took away your camp. How'd you know I went and spoke to them? I never told you."

He didn't move.

I said, "You told them that Dad tells me his secrets, right? That's why they've been hounding me."

"I didn't," he screamed. He sounded close to tears.

"Maybe you didn't speak to the FBI," I said. "But you spoke to *someone,* didn't you? Because they promised you that camp, didn't they? Whoever you told, told the FBI. You know what? I'm glad they took your camp away!"

Bobby spun around. His face was so twisted I couldn't tell if he was angry or about to burst a gut. He said, "You idiot! You have no idea how the world works, do you?"

I said, "Who did you talk to?"

"That's for me to know and you to find out. Get out of here. I can't wait to leave this family."

I lay on my bed, struggling to put things together. Far as I was concerned, Bobby had admitted he'd made a deal with someone to get into that summer camp. That someone talked to the FBI. So who was that someone?

In all the detective stories I ever read, near the end, the private eye seems stumped. Then he goes over everything that happened, all the facts, all the clues, and *blam!* he gets his answer.

I went over everything as much as I could remember, the way hard-boiled detectives did, Sam Spade style. Then I remembered something Mr. Ordson had said: "In an age of suspicion the last people we suspect is ourselves."

So for the first time I tried to think what *I* had done.

And gradually, very gradually—just the way it worked in the stories—I came to know who the informer was.

"Jeez Louise," I said, like Al Depaco did. It actually made sense. All of it.

I had figured it out.

But what was I going to do about it?

Doughnut.

The following Wednesday, June 27, was a really hot day for the end of June. Dad came home late. I knew where he'd been even though we had never talked about his brother since that night after the movie. Right after he showed up we all sat down to dinner. No one was talking. Everyone seemed glum, especially Dad.

"What is it, honey?" Ma asked him. "Something at the college?"

He looked at her. "Someone I know is very ill. I was just thinking about him." He sent her an eye message.

We all stopped eating.

Bobby said, "Who is it?"

"A fellow by the name of Nelson Kasper. Nobody you know."

Bobby stared at his plate.

Ma put a hand to her throat. "How is he doing?"

"Very poorly," said Dad.

After dinner, Dad went to his office. Ma joined him briefly, then went to the radio room to listen to some classical music and work on her photo scrapbooks.

Bobby got on the phone.

I went to my room and picked up my *Detective Magazine*. In the table of contents were stories titled "Goodbye Forever" and "You Only Live Once." I decided to read one called "The Red Silk Scarf."

"Pete . . ."

I opened my eyes. I had fallen asleep reading. Dad was bending over me. "Pete," he whispered again. "I need you."

"What's happened?"

"I'll tell you on the way. Don't wake Bobby."

I was already dressed. Dad was waiting in the hallway. Ma was there in her bathrobe. She gave Dad a hug, then me. "Thanks for helping Dad," she said into my ear.

"What's happening?" I said, befuddled.

"Dad will tell you."

"What is it?" I asked as Dad and I waited for the elevator.

"My brother," Dad said. "Got a call from the nursing home. I need to be there. Come on."

"Is he dying?"

Dad nodded.

"What time is it?"

"About two thirty."

Dad and I stepped out of our building. The air was humid, thick as cotton. A taxi was waiting. We climbed in and Dad told the driver where to go. The taxi sped through the deserted streets, the red and green stoplights looking like last year's Christmas decorations.

I said, "Why did you want me to come?"

"I don't want to get your ma involved. She's never seen Frank, and the less she knows about him the better. And Bobby doesn't know anything."

I thought, *Yes he does.*

Dad said, "I might need some help and you're the only other person who knows about him."

As we went over the Brooklyn Bridge, I peeked out the rear window. A car was behind us, but I told myself it didn't matter. Instead, I tried to think what my dad was thinking. Was he glad or sorry Frank was dying? Was he blaming himself? Was he happy I was with him, or was I only there because Dad couldn't ask anyone else?

We reached the nursing home and got out of the cab. A high, solitary lamp lit the deserted street. A street-washing truck must have just gone by, because the pavement glistened with blackness. The only other light came from inside the glass doors of the nursing home.

Dad found a call button by the doorway and pushed it. In moments, the door opened a couple of inches. A woman looked out. She was wearing a white jacket and had a stethoscope around her neck and a clipboard in one hand. From the clipboard dangled a stubby yellow pencil on a string.

"Mr. Collison?"

"Yes, thanks for calling me, Dr. Porter."

The doctor pushed the door open.

As we walked in, Dad asked, "How is he?"

"As I told you on the phone," she said, "Mr. Kasper's

condition has seriously worsened. Just come this way."
As she started down the hall, I heard the door lock click
behind us.

My dad started to follow, only to stop. He looked at
me. "Do you want to come or wait here?" He turned to
the doctor. "My son."

The doctor said, "Your decision."

Dad shifted back to me.

"I'll come."

"Fine."

As we walked down the hallway, the doctor said to
Dad, "I know you're Mr. Kasper's custodian. What exactly
is your relationship to him?"

"He's my war buddy."

"It's hard to believe he's as young as you told us."

"A very hard life," said Dad.

"Mr. Collison," said the doctor. "I wanted to ask . . . I
had instructions to call you if your friend's health turned
critical. Which, of course, I've done. Earlier this evening
there was a request from someone who told us that he was
Mr. Kasper's relative."

Dad halted. "Who was it?"

The doctor checked her clipboard. "A Mr. Smith."

Dad looked at me. I knew his thought: The FBI.

Dad said, "Did you call him?"

"I wanted to talk to you first."

"Best not call," said Dad. "Not yet."

"As you wish," said the doctor.

The doctor opened the door and stepped away. Dad started in, but paused to look a question at me. I nodded. He made a small movement with his head. I followed him inside.

There was enough light to see Uncle Frank lying under a white blanket. Nothing about him looked like family. His eyes were closed, his mouth partly open. He had no teeth. Over his chest, which barely moved, lay one clawlike hand, with cracked fingernails. How could someone so young look so old?

Dad went up to the bed and bent over. "Frank," he said, "it's me, Denny. I'm with you." There was no response. Dad kissed his brother's forehead. When Dad stood up again, he was holding his brother's hand.

I crept closer. Hardly knowing what to think, or feel, I tried guessing what Dad felt. He'd told me that Frank had always listened to him. Was he sorry now for telling Frank to go away? Had he missed him all these years? Are you still a brother if your brother disappears? Not knowing what else to do, I took Dad's other hand.

I don't know how long we were standing there when I realized the doctor was beside us.

She whispered, "You were just in time. I'm afraid he's gone."

Dad let out a long, low breath, gazed at his brother, and kissed him on his forehead again. When he straightened up, he said, "I'm glad he's at peace."

I gazed at the man on the bed. I'd never seen death

before, not for real. Even as I looked at it, it didn't make sense.

Dad, his voice quiet and controlled, told me he had some arrangements to make, and asked me to wait for him in the lobby. As I walked back, the hallway seemed to have become a lot longer.

The lobby was deserted, like an empty shell you might find on a beach, just bigger. I sat on the couch and tried to make sense of what I had seen, of what had happened. Dad had lost his brother for a second time. I'd lost an uncle I never had.

As I sat there, I gazed at the picture of the mountains, wondering if the moon looked like that. Bobby wanted to go to the moon. Did he really want to go there, or did he just want to get away from us? Would I lose my brother?

I tried to grasp how I felt about Bobby. Did he really hate our family? Me? I worried that if I told Dad what Bobby had done, Dad would get angry and Bobby would disappear—like Frank. It would be my fault. I didn't like Bobby, but I didn't want him to go. Maybe someday we could be friends. But the only way that could happen was if I kept what he did a secret.

Next thing I knew Dad was waking me with a shoulder shake. I looked up at him. He was carrying a small bundle and a checkerboard. I looked at the bundle.

He said, "The few things my brother owned. This is it." He sat down next to me. He seemed worn out.

"I'm sorry," I said, wishing I had a better word.

"Thanks. Poor Frank. What a short, miserable life." Dad rubbed his mustache. "And death doesn't explain itself, does it? Glad I was able to help at the end . . . a little."

I said, "Was he in that Soviet prison a long time?"

Dad nodded. "Do you know what he said was the hardest part?"

"What?"

"Knowing who he was and finding ways to be true to himself somewhere, inside. Even if you're not in prison, staying true to your own thoughts is hard." Dad was silent for a moment and then he said, "Let me tell you, Pal, grown-ups lose their freedom a lot. And they don't have to be in prison."

I remembered how, just a short time ago, I felt like I'd stopped being a kid. Sitting there, I wanted to be one again.

I said, "Did you call Ma?"

He nodded.

"Going to tell Bobby?"

"I will. Sometime."

"The rest of your family?"

"Same." He yawned. "In a couple of weeks there will be another family gathering."

"We have to go?"

He closed his eyes for a second, then opened them. "Hey, Pal, families are like ghosts. You may not believe in them but they haunt you anyway."

"Who do you think that 'Mr. Smith' was?"

He said, "I'm hoping it no longer matters. Frank doesn't have to pretend anymore." He closed his eyes. Rubbed them.

"One good thing," he said. "That hearing, the committee investigation, it's July fourteenth."

"Why is that good?"

"Because if they ask me about Frank, it no longer matters."

"Dad . . . What's going to happen?"

He shrugged.

I looked up at him and said, "I'm glad you're my father."

"Thanks, Pal," he said. He reached out and squeezed my hand, then drifted into his own thoughts.

After a moment he said, "Hey, do me a favor and see if there are any cabs out there."

I got up and pushed open one of the doors. I stepped onto the sidewalk. The early-morning light was thin and drowsy, as if the day were having trouble getting up. I didn't see any taxis. What I did see, parked just down the street, was the gray Chevy.

I spun around and pulled at the nursing home door. It was locked. When I pressed my face against the pebbled glass, I couldn't see through. I was about to ring the bell, but I looked down the street again. The Chevy was just sitting there. The face behind the windshield was dim, but I had no doubt it was the informer. I wanted to be sure.

I walked down the street, expecting the car to drive off.

When I reached the car, the driver-side window was open. Sitting there, just as I expected, was Uncle Chris. Bobby had been talking to him, and Chris had been telling the FBI what he said.

As I stood there looking at him, it was hard to know

which I felt more, satisfaction that I'd solved the case, or hatred for him.

Chris said, "My brother die?"

I shook my head.

His voice a little embarrassed, he said, "Bobby called me. Said Tom was dying."

I said, "It wasn't Tom. It was an army friend of my father's. Nelson Kasper. From the state of Washington." I turned back toward the nursing home.

Uncle Chris came halfway out of his car. "Come on, Pete. Who was he?"

I kept walking.

When I reached the nursing home, I banged on the door. As I did, the black Ford pulled up to the curb. Ewing jumped out. "Hey, Pete! Hold it!"

I rang the bell. "Dad!" I called. "Come quick!"

Dad started to come out. I blocked his way and pushed him back. Soon as I got in, I yanked the door shut behind me.

"What's the matter?" he said.

The doorbell rang. I grabbed Dad's arm, getting him to move toward the hallway. "We gotta go this way," I said.

"Why? What's going on?"

"Just come." I was dragging him.

The bell kept ringing.

Dad said, "What's going on? Where are we going?"

"Tell you when we get there."

As I hurried him down the hallway, the doctor scooted by, heading toward the front door.

At the far end of the hall was that door marked EXIT. I pushed it open.

"Come on," I said to Dad, yanking at him.

"Pete . . ."

"Please!"

We went down the short flight of steps, where I shoved open the door to the outside. We were in the alley.

"Where are we?" said Dad.

"Behind the nursing home. This way." I was still hauling on him.

"Will you tell me what's going on."

"Later."

We got to the street and kept going. After a couple of blocks, we turned east, where I knew I'd find a subway.

Dad halted. "Pete, I need you to tell me what this is all about."

If I told him about Chris, I would have had to tell him about Bobby. But I wasn't Sam Spade. I couldn't turn him in. All I said was, "Ewing was out front."

"The FBI? Are you serious? Do they know about my brother?"

"Not sure."

Dad was silent for a few moments. "Okay," he said. "I guess it doesn't matter anymore. Let's go home."

The Giants celebrated the Fourth of July by playing Brooklyn a doubleheader and losing both games. But on

July 10, there was this story in the *Times* that I read and reread:

DASHIELL HAMMETT JAILED IN RED BAIT INQUIRY

Dashiell Hammett, author of "The Maltese Falcon" and "The Thin Man," and chairman of an organization calling itself the Civil Rights Congress, which is designated by the attorney general as a Communist subversive front, was convicted yesterday of criminal contempt for refusing to divulge the names of those in his organization. Sentenced to six months in jail, he was taken to the Federal House of Detention.

Dad had told us he would refuse to give names. Did that mean he would go to jail, too?

40

On July 14, Dad's hearing was held in the Foley Square Courthouse in lower Manhattan. It was a gigantic building, with massive four-story columns in front. To me it looked like the Brooklyn Borough Hall's big brother.

Dad had given Bobby and me the choice to come or not. But he said, "It would be nice to have my family with me." We went.

We got there early morning—Dad, Ma, Bobby, Dad's lawyer, Mr. Miller, and me. Morning, but already so hot, it made sitting home in the fridge a cool thought. All types of people were going in and out of the courthouse while a small army of cops and security guards were hanging around, pistols on their belts.

We stepped into a gigantic circular lobby, three levels high. All round the high ceilings were paintings of people. Dad pointed up and said, "The great lawgivers of the world." The only faces I recognized were Washington's and Lincoln's.

Ma said, "Your dad and I got our marriage license here. Cost three dollars."

Dad grinned. "A bargain."

Dad's lawyer led us to a large room whose walls were covered with wood panels. Up front was a long table covered with a green cloth. Some padded chairs stood behind it. An American flag as well as the flags of New York State and the City were on poles. On the wall was a clock with Roman numerals. Facing the long table was a smaller table, with two folding chairs behind it. What the room had, mostly, was silence. But it felt powerful. I felt small.

Someone was placing pitchers of iced water on the tables, along with glasses. Behind the smaller table were rows of chairs, half of them full. Bobby whispered that some of the occupants were newspaper reporters. We sat there, too.

A little after nine o'clock, a few official-looking people—suits too big for them—came in and sat down at that long table. One of the men banged a gavel on a block of wood and said, "I think we can begin. The subcommittee will be in order. My name is Chairman Kierman."

He seemed dignified and sure of himself.

Mr. Kierman read from some papers. "This committee

is continuing a series of hearings respecting the counter-attack by the Communist conspiracy in the United States against part of our government's programs, the work of the congressional committee to expose the Communist operations."

He went on and on, never looking up. I tried to make sense of what he was saying. That wasn't easy, because he spoke for about forty-five minutes about how Communists were working to undermine the United States, and how it was all directed by Soviet rulers, particularly Stalin. He said that Communists had snuck into various organizations, local governments, even schools, and that they were all eager to overthrow the country.

Scary stuff, it reminded me of what Mr. Donavan used to say. I kept telling myself Dad had nothing to do with it.

The chairman called someone's name. Two men went up to the small table and sat down.

The chairman said, "Will you raise your right hand. Do you swear the testimony you are about to give will be the truth, the whole truth, and nothing but the truth, so help you God?"

One of the guys said, "I do." The other man must have been his lawyer.

"Please identify yourself by name, residence, and occupation," said the chairman.

"My name is Abner Brown. I live at Four Sixty East Thirty-seventh Street, New York City, New York. As to my occupation, I decline to answer on the ground that this committee has no authority to conduct this inquiry and is violating my rights under the First Amendment and my privileges under the Fifth Amendment not to be a witness against myself."

"Just a minute," said the chairman. "What trouble do you think you would get into if you stated your occupation?"

"I decline to answer that for the reasons I just stated."

"Are you ashamed of your occupation?"

The guy leaned over and talked to his lawyer. Then he said, "Not at all."

"Then state it," the chairman pushed.

"I decline for the reasons I just stated, sir," said the man.

"You are appearing today, Mr. Brown, in response to a subpoena, which was served upon you by this Senate committee about activities which may be deemed un-American. Is that correct?" asked the chairman.

"Yes, sir."

From there they kept asking him questions, and he kept refusing to answer for the reasons he already gave.

I whispered to Dad, "Why won't he answer anything?"

"The law says, if he answers one thing he has to answer everything."

It seemed like a stage play without any action.

Eventually the man was told to step down, and someone else took his place, a woman this time. The same kind of back-and-forth questions happened all over again. She kept refusing to answer, too.

This went on for a couple of hours, until the chairman called out, "The committee calls Mr. Dennis Collison to the witness table."

I sat up very straight.

Dad looked at Ma, who gave him a tight smile, and then he went to sit at the table with his lawyer. I checked around the room. That's when I saw Ewing sitting there. He saw me and waved.

I didn't wave back.

The chairman said, "Will you raise your right hand. Do you swear the testimony you are about to give will be the truth, the whole truth, and nothing but the truth, so help you God?"

"I do."

"Please identify yourself by name, residence, and occupation."

"My name is Dennis Collison. I live at One Forty-five Hicks Street, Brooklyn, New York. I teach American history at New City College."

"How long have you been teaching there?"

"Six years."

"Do you have a specialty?"

"The American Revolution."

"So you have particular interest in revolutions?"

"It's how our country began."

"The committee has been given information that you were a member of the Communist Party."

"I was."

"Thank you for your honesty. When?"

"It was in 1934. I went to one meeting. I was nineteen years old."

"Why did you join?"

"I don't think you have the right to ask me that. If you think I have committed a crime, the lawful authorities can bring charges against me."

"You are now required to answer."

"I won't do it."

"On what grounds?"

"It's not the government's business to ask what I think."

"By answering questions you have already waived your right not to answer. Please tell us the names of those with whom you attended meetings of the Communist Party."

"I only went to one meeting. I won't tell you who was there."

"You can be held in contempt of Congress."

"I won't give you names."

"You may go to jail."

"I intend to hold on to my own thoughts."

"Even if it is a conspiracy against the United States of America?"

"If I have broken laws you can prosecute me. I will not be a party to prosecuting people because of their political convictions."

"We have information that your father, Thomas Collison, went to the Soviet Union in 1934. Why did he go?"

"To find work."

"Was he a Communist?"

"No."

"Where is he now?"

"He died."

"Died?" The man seemed surprised.

"Yes, sir."

"Do you have any written proof of that?"

"No."

"Who informed you?"

"A member of my family."

"Very well. Now you also had a brother, Frank Collison. He too went to the Soviet Union, with your father. Tell us what happened to him."

"I refuse."

"On what grounds?"

"Because I hold these truths to be self-evident, that all men—"

"Mr. Collison, please answer the question."

"—are created equal, that they are endowed by their Creator—"

"You are out of order, Mr. Collison."

"—with certain unalienable rights—"

"You are in contempt of Congress, Mr. Collison."

"That among these are life, liberty and the pursuit of happiness."

"Mr. Collison, you may be sent to prison. Again, do you know what happened to your brother?"

"You heard my answer."

The man leaned over and whispered to the man sitting next to him. Then the chairman looked at the clock, banged his gavel down, and said, "Witness dismissed."

I was proud of my dad. But I was also fearful that he might still be in trouble.

We headed out of the court. As we were passing through the doors, I felt a tap on my shoulder. I turned around. It was Ewing.

He said, "Hey, Pete, who was that dead guy?"

I stood there, looking at him, unable to think of something to say, when Dad came forward. "Who are you, sir?"

"Special Agent Ewing, FBI."

Dad said, "Do you know what they call people who try to intimidate kids?"

Ewing looked startled, but said nothing.

"Cowards," said Dad.

41

That night at dinner, Dad said, "You all should know I won't be returning to my college. They learned about my hearing and asked me what I intended to say. When I told them I wouldn't cooperate, they said I was not welcome back."

I said, "Didn't they care why you kept your mouth shut?"

"Nope," said Dad.

"You hate them?" Bobby asked.

"I'm sad, mostly. And disappointed."

"Dad," I asked quietly, "you going to jail?"

Dad looked at me. "Don't know."

"You've lost your job and everything is all messed up," said Bobby. "What are we going to do?"

"We'll do what people always do. Try to survive. Find a way. Try to live a normal life."

Ma said, "For instance, we have a family party this Sunday."

"Do we have to go?" Bobby asked.

"Absolutely. We can practice being ourselves."

On Sunday, when I got up, I found that the Giants, having been beaten by the Cubs, had dropped to third place. But mostly I was thinking about the family gathering. About seeing Uncle Chris.

It was hot and humid when we took the subway to Aunt Shirley's place. She lived in the bottom apartment of a brownstone building in Park Slope, Brooklyn. I was worried. Would people say something mean to Dad?

The same people were there, from Grandma in a corner, already knitting, to my little cousin Toby. He was in a cowboy costume, shooting everybody with a cap pistol.

When we walked in, I was sure all the grown-ups looked at Dad in a different way. People were quieter than usual. I felt tension. I kept my eyes on Uncle Chris. He had his eyes on Dad. When he saw me looking at him, he moved away.

Dad went up to Grandma and kissed her cheek. He said a few words and then went on to other relatives. I don't know what he said to Grandma, but it was clear to me that he hadn't said anything to her about Frank.

My cousin Ralph got a bunch of cousins to play Clue. I wasn't interested but played anyway. We were playing in a room that overlooked a little outside yard, where Uncle Chris was sitting in a chair. He had his *Daily Worker* in front of him, like a billboard. Or a challenge.

I dropped my marker—I had been Professor Plum—and announced, "I'm out. Got to speak to Uncle Chris."

Ignoring protests, I went out the back. At first, Uncle Chris acted as if he didn't see me. I stood before him. He looked up. We stared at each other.

"You tell your father I was there?" he asked.

I said, "All those years ago, when my grandfather disappeared, you knew where he went, didn't you?"

"Hey, back then, Russia was the future. Far as I can tell, still is. He was smart to go."

"Why didn't you go?"

"I should have. But the Party had work for me here, getting people to join up. You believe in something, you work with your comrades. When they ask you to do a job, you do it."

I said, "My father ran away so he could be different from the family, so he could go to school. And to get away from you."

"Yeah. Dennis always thought he was better than his family. Still does. Forgets where he comes from. Ran off without telling his mother. Disgusting. She wanted to know where Dennis and Frank went. I found out about Tom, too—not Frank. When your grandma heard where Tom went, do you know what she said?"

I shook my head.

"She said, 'I refuse to believe it.'"

"You found out Dad joined the Communist Party."

Chris shrugged. "One meeting. He should have gone to more. He would have learned more than from those books he read."

I said, "You're working with the FBI, aren't you?"

"Who told you that?"

"I figured it out myself."

He gazed at me, a slight smile on his lips. "Regular detective, aren't you? Okay. A few years ago, I got into a little trouble about taxes. Small mistakes. But the feds knew about my politics and said if I gave them info, they'd go easy. Hey, sometimes enemies can cooperate. Look at World War Two, Russia and the U.S. So sure, I give the FBI names—names of stupid people, people who don't matter, wishy-washy liberals like your father. Figured I'd keep the FBI interested in little fish and they'd leave me and my comrades alone."

I said, "But Dad's your nephew."

"I wanted to teach Dennis which side he should have been on."

"And you dragged Bobby in."

"Bobby's smart. He wants to get into that rocket camp. Good for him. I tell him I got contacts in the government. Give me some info about your old man and I'll see what I can do. Bobby says, 'Pete is Dad's favorite. Tells him everything.' I say to Bobby, 'There you go. We find out stuff from Pete and you got yourself a deal.'

"Then all of a sudden you come along and start asking questions about my brother Tom. You ask Grandma questions. You ask me. You're like some stupid junior detective. I gave you the name of that idiot, Al Depaco, to see if you'd ask him. You did. I'm thinking, what's going on? Why is this kid asking all these questions about my brother? Maybe Tom turned on Russia and came back to America. Dennis knows and tells Pete. Hey, if I can find out about Tom, and tell the FBI, I'll be their hero and all my problems disappear."

I stood there, hardly believing how selfish—and wrong—he was. "You made Dad lose his job," I said.

"For a good cause."

"What cause? You?"

"Nothing to do with *me*," he said with indignation. "I'm a Communist and proud of it. The last thing my side needs is for old Tom to come back here and tell people lies about the Soviet Union. I don't want that to happen. Hey, your dad turned his back on what he believed. And his family. He's getting what he deserves. Thanks to me, the FBI wastes time on him. A nobody.

"They check your school. Talk to your teacher. Checked to see where you were going Thursdays. The blind guy. That time I called, you said you were going to visit your father at school. I got them to follow you. A nursing home. Big break! Maybe Tom is there.

"Then what do you do? You go to Ewing, tell him you

know who I am. Hey, I don't want anyone knowing I'm working with the FBI, do I? I thought, I'll scare the kid a little. And it works. You tell Ewing you won't say anything."

He disgusted me more and more.

But he went on. "You know what, Communism is the future. What future you got that's better than that?"

I said, "I won't let anyone tell me what to think."

"You're a kid! What do you know about thinking? All I want to know is, you going to tell all this stuff to Dennis?"

"Doughnut."

"What's that supposed to mean?" he called after me, because by then I had walked away.

I had two thoughts: how much I hated Uncle Chris, and how I had been right about everything.

I went and found my dad. "I'm feeling sick," I said. "I think I need to go home."

"We could find a place for you to lie down here."

I shook my head.

"Okay," he said, "I'll take you. Mom and Bobby can stay, make our apologies."

We got out onto the street.

"Need a taxi?" he asked.

"I'm fine."

"I thought you were sick."

"Didn't want to stay."

Dad considered me. "Let's go to the park," he said. When we got there, we sat down on a bench.

Dad said, "Guess what? When your Uncle Mort heard I lost my teaching job, he offered me a position with his insurance company."

"You going to take it?"

"Funny, in a way. I'm a historian," he said. "I've spent a lot of time dealing with the past. By selling insurance, I have to work on the future. I guess I can do it."

I sat there thinking how complicated families were. Uncle Mort being nice. Uncle Chris, rotten. And Bobby . . . I was still mad at him, but I just couldn't tell Dad about what he had done.

"Dad," I said, "I don't like Bobby. Don't know what to do about it."

"Hey, Pal, you only have one brother. And older brothers have it hard."

"How?"

"We think we always have to be better, smarter. But we aren't. Older brothers need help now and then. Try to be nice to him."

I said, "You know what the Giants' manager said?"

Dad shook his head.

"'Nice guys finish last.'"

"Hope he's wrong." Dad laughed as he put his arm around my shoulder. "Hey, Pal, we're going to be okay."

That night it was so hot and sticky humid, I found it hard to sleep. On his side of the room, I could hear Bobby thrashing about.

Then he said, "It's all so stupid."

"What are you talking about?" I said.

"Dad. He's lost his job. Maybe he'll go to jail. All because he went to a Communist Party meeting years ago."

Then I said, "And because of you."

He was silent for a moment. Then he said, "What do you mean?"

"I know you talked to Uncle Chris."

Bobby appeared at the edge of the partition. He glared at me, his lean face full of anger.

I said, "The FBI told Uncle Chris they'd get you into that rocket camp if you told him things about Dad."

"Not true," he cried.

"Yes it is. I just talked to Uncle Chris. He told me I'm right."

I felt like Sam Spade laying out the truth, the truth that hurts somebody.

The tightness left him. He seemed to go limp, like dead flowers in old water. For a long time he just stood there, then he said, "You tell Dad? About me? Uncle Chris?"

Remembering what Dad told me all those weeks ago I said, "Pal, if you don't take some wrong turns, you aren't going anywhere."

"Where'd you get that?"

All I said was, "I'll make a deal with you."

"What?"

"If I promise not to tell Dad or Ma what you did, you have to promise not to run off."

He actually seemed to have to think that through. "I am going away to college," he said.

I said, "I can't wait for that."

He went back to his side.

"Hey, Bobby."

"What?"

I said, "I'm a Giants fan. You're a Dodger fan. But you're still my brother."

It took a while for him to call out, "Pete."

"What?"

"Thanks."

I never told Dad about Bobby. Or Uncle Chris. I didn't turn Bobby in. I wasn't Sam Spade.

But this story doesn't end here. A miracle was about to happen.

A fter that family get-together, I went back to Mr. Ord-son's and told him what had happened.

"You truly are a detective," he said. He actually grinned.

"Yeah. Me and Sam Spade."

"A fine partnership."

Loki wagged his tail.

But I wouldn't talk politics.

Dad started to work for Uncle Mort. Ma didn't take the summer off the way she used to. Bobby got a summer job at some electronics company. He was mostly running errands and fetching coffee. But he told us he was learning about the future, something called "computers." I had no idea what they were and didn't care.

I got a job too, at Ritman's Books. Every morning I opened the store, emptied Mr. Ritman's ashtray, swept the sidewalk, sold a few things, sat behind the counter, and read mysteries. I didn't smoke.

In the afternoons, I listened to ball games, every Giants game. I knew Russ Hodges's voice—the Giants' announcer's—as well as my own.

Summer seemed to last forever. It was hot and sticky, with not much to do. No friends. I just kept reading. Hammett. Chandler. Macdonald.

Ma took just two weeks for vacation. Ritman gave me time off. Ma and I took a Greyhound Bus to Indiana, where we spent time with her family.

I got to know my cousins a bit. They were okay. They rooted for the Cincinnati Reds, like Ewing.

On August 8 I picked up Ma's afternoon paper and read the top story.

Senator McCarthy said today he intends to give the Senate tomorrow the names of twenty-nine past or present employees of the State Department whose loyalties have been questioned. "Some very high officials are on the list," Senator McCarthy said.

The next day I got a coded letter from Kat.

dear traitor i am in maine at girls camp silver lake okay fun stuff sometimes but no punch ball

pounds of mosquitoes and black flies my mother
said i can come back to the city and live with
her when i start high school hope you will be
there what high school will you go write to
me dodgers k

I wrote back in code.

dear angel my life is very boring but i learned everything will tell you if i ever see you again wish
i could see you now city hot when you come back
will you live in the neighborhood miss you a lot
giants p

On August 11, the Giants were thirteen and a half games
behind the Dodgers. *Thirteen and a half games behind!*

That's when the miracle began to happen.

On August 12, the Giants beat Philadelphia in both
games of the Sunday doubleheader. Then they kept winning. Every game. By August 26, they were only five games
behind Brooklyn.

On September 1, they beat Brooklyn, and did it with
a triple play.

After Labor Day, I began school again, the eighth
grade. Mr. Donavan had left PS 10. I had no idea where
he went. My new teacher was Mr. Malakowski, although
he told us to call him Mr. Mal. He was easygoing, and really liked baseball. He didn't talk politics.

Early on, one of the kids raised his hands. "Mr. Mal, Mr. Donavan used to tell us war stories. You got any?"

Mr. Mal said, "I don't know what Mr. Donavan told you. But I have to tell you, he never was in the army. No idea where he got his stories. Maybe the movies. Me, I'd just as soon forget all that. I'm just happy to be alive and with you all."

There were some kids from my old class in Mr. Mal's room, but all that Commie stuff seemed to have been melted away. The talk was mostly about Dodgers and Giants. Because the other kids knew I was a Giants fan, things got fun. Razzing, teasing, and joking.

I was the only Giants fan in my class. In fact, I think I was the only Giants fan in the whole school. Maybe the only one in Brooklyn. I was famous for not being like everybody else. I loved it.

By September 22, with the Giants still winning and the Dodgers still losing, we would start each day talking about what was happening in the standings. People were getting crazy.

On September 28, the Giants tied the Dodgers for first place.

That weekend, each team had only two games to play.

The Giants won both of theirs. So did Brooklyn, though in the last Dodger game it took a home run by Jackie Robinson to win in the fourteenth inning.

That meant the Giants and the Dodgers had to have a play-off series, best of three.

No one talked about anything else except the play-offs. In school, Mr. Mal brought in a radio, and when the games came on in the afternoon, we just sat at our desks and listened to every inning of every game. If the game was still going on at three o'clock—and they did—we just stayed in school. No one left. That had never happened before.

In the play-offs, the Giants won the first of the games. Then the Dodgers won the second.

It all came down to one, last game on October 3.

The game was played at the Polo Grounds, the Giants' field. It was a warm, humid day. For the Giants, Sal Maglie was the starter. For the Dodgers, Don Newcombe. Both were ace pitchers. Each had won twenty games.

At the end of the fifth inning, the Dodgers were winning one—zip.

By the end of the sixth, the Giants had gotten one run. So the game was tied, one—one.

In the seventh, the Dodgers went ahead by three runs.

The Giants came to bat at the bottom of the ninth, down by three.

Al Dark, the Giants' captain, led off with a base hit.

Don Mueller, next up, got another single that sent Dark to third.

Monte Irvin, the Giants' best hitter, was up next. Straining for a home run, the tying run, he popped up, for an easy out.

Whitey Lockman, the first baseman, came to the plate. He got a double. Dark scored. Mueller got to third.

The score was now Dodgers four, Giants two.

The Dodgers' manager, Chuck Dressen, changed pitchers, bringing in Ralph Branca. Branca had a nickname, Honk, short for Honker, because some people thought he had a big nose.

Bobby Thomson came to the plate for the Giants.

Branca threw a fastball. Strike one.

The whole class was going crazy, shouting, hooting, and banging desks. Mr. Mal was laughing right along.

The next pitch came in high and inside. Bobby Thomson swung. The announcer, Russ Hodges, said it all:

There's a long drive . . . it's gonna be . . . I believe—the Giants win the pennant! The Giants win the pennant! The Giants win the pennant! The Giants win the pennant! Bobby Thomson hits one into the lower deck of the left-field stands and they are going crazy. I don't believe it! I don't believe it!

I was going crazy, too.

The next day, October 4, the newspaper headlines read

GIANTS CAPTURE PENNANT, BEATING DODGERS 5–4 IN 9TH ON THOMSON'S 3-RUN HOMER IT'S LIKE A FUNERAL IN BROOKLYN

All I could think was, I had to see Kat.

That week at Mr. Ordson's, we were talking about the game and the bet Kat and I had made.

"What's happened to Kat?" he asked.

"Still in boarding school."

"Where is it?"

"Westport, Connecticut."

"Not so very far," he said.

That night I asked Dad if he had an atlas. He gave it to me and I looked to see where Westport was. Mr. Ordson was right. It wasn't far from Brooklyn. I started thinking about a visit.

43

A few days later, my parents were reading in the radio room when I walked in and said, "On Saturday, I'm taking the train to Connecticut and going to see Kat. At her school."

Dad and Ma talked with their eyes.

"That's wonderful," said Ma. "Who are you going with?"

"Going alone."

Dad and Ma exchanged more looks. Dad said, "Do you know how?"

I said, "IRT to Times Square. Shuttle to Grand Central. Nine a.m. New Haven Railroad to Westport. Taxi to Blessed Saint Anne's School for Girls."

Ma said, "How'd you learn all that?"

"A librarian with crinkly eyes."

Ma said, "I'd be happy to go with you."

"Want to do it alone."

"Does she know you're coming?"

"Going to surprise her. The Giants won and we had a bet."

Dad laughed and my parents agreed to let me go after I wrote out all the directions and phone numbers for them in case something came up.

That night I hardly slept.

I got up, put on the Giants sweatshirt Dad gave me, and was on the subway by seven. Went to Grand Central Station. Bought a ticket to Westport, and asked ten thousand people the right way. I was the first one on the train to New Haven that left at 9:00.

A conductor came by. When I handed him my ticket, I said, "Will you tell me when we get to Westport?"

"I'll shout it out, sonny."

Which is what he did.

I got off the train and walked out of the station. Outside was a line of taxis. I went to the first one, and said, "Can you take me to Blessed Saint Anne's School for Girls?"

"Three bucks."

I showed him the money.

We drove into the country. The leaves were green and golden, and the sky was so blue, the city felt like a memory.

Twenty minutes later the cab went through large rusty iron gates, up to a big stone building that looked more like a castle than a school. After I paid him, the driver handed me a smudged card. "If you need a ride back to the station, call this number. Ask for Harry."

He drove off. I walked up the wide castle stairs into a lobby where an older girl was sitting behind an old wood table. She was dressed in a green school jacket with a white blouse and a plaid tie.

"Can I help you?"

"I'm looking for Katherine Boyer," I said. "I'm a friend."

"What grade is she in?"

"Eighth."

"Eights have team practice Saturday mornings. Do you know her sport?"

I was about to say punchball, but shook my head.

She said, "Probably field hockey. Just go out to the back fields. You'll find her." She pointed the way.

I wandered around until I found a big field. It was full of girls in plaid skirts and white shirts, running around in circles. They carried funny-looking sticks with a bend at the bottom, which they used to whack a ball along the ground—upside-down baseball.

I stood and watched. Then I saw Kat. She was wearing a short plaid skirt like everyone else. Her legs were dirty, her white shirt's tails were pulled out, but her hair was tied back with a string. She was wearing a blue Dodgers sweatshirt.

As she ran, one hand held her stick, her other hand kept pushing up her glasses. She was heading down the side of the field, near where I was standing.

When she got close, I called, "Hey, angel!"

Kat stopped and spun in my direction, just stood there and stared. Next moment she flung down her stick and ran toward me, only to stop again three feet away. She said, "Hello, traitor."

I said, "Hey, sweetheart! Giants won!"

Kat, with a grin as big and warm as the first real day in spring, said, "Wait till next year."

And just like that, I felt like a kid again.

Author's Note

History is memory researched. Historical fiction is memory brought to life.

Catch You Later, Traitor comes from many sources, moments that others or I lived. Its true origin can be located some thirty years ago, when I met a man who told me how he had gone to the Soviet Union as a teenager with his father. His story is very like Tom Collison and Frank's, who go there in this novel. In that man's case, he and his father were lucky enough to return to the United States in 1939. They had come home to convince his mother and brother to join them in Russia. However, World War Two broke out and he never returned. His fascinating story stayed in my mind.

A full and tragic account of those who went to the Soviet Union to find work—and never returned—may be read in *The Forsaken* by Tim Tzouliadis.

It was in 1951, as a boy growing up in Brooklyn, New York (I was thirteen at the time), that I switched my baseball allegiance from the Brooklyn Dodgers to the New York Giants, my own Declaration of Independence. It was a glorious year to have done so, for the Giants did indeed win the pennant in that extraordinary play-off series with the Dodgers. The next day the headline, "It's Like a Funeral in Brooklyn," appeared in the *New York Times*. You can read about that season in *The Miracle at Coogan's Bluff* by Thomas Kiernan.

As a boy, I did have a weekly job of reading newspapers to a blind man, a Mr. Smith. The availability of the job was announced during one of my weekly Boy Scout meetings. I wish I could remember his dog's name.

I do not recall when I first read *The Maltese Falcon*. The book and its author, Dashiell Hammett, made an enormous impression on me as a reader and a writer. The book is quite extraordinary, and the film version (with Humphrey Bogart) is almost as good. Hammett's work led me to other hard-boiled American writers, Raymond Chandler, Ross Macdonald, among many. I would be honored to think they influenced my writing. My hope here is that Pete Collison, in his narrative, has managed to honor the style and words of the books he, and I, loved to read—and still read.

As a kid, one could not live in New York City in the 1950s without knowing people caught up in the political turmoil of the time. Yes, it was an astonishing year for baseball, but the Korean War was raging, Truman fired General MacArthur, Senator McCarthy was ascendant, *The Adventures of Sam Spade, Detective* was taken off the radio airwaves, and Dashiell Hammett was sent to jail for refusing to divulge names of Communist sympathizers, names, it would appear, he did not even know.

My account of the Subversive Activities Control Board hearing is based on contemporaneous congressional transcripts.

Public school, punchball, inkwells, Communists and anti-Communists, blacklisting, Mr. Donavan and Mr. Mal, are all very real in my memory. The titles of the short story mystery tales and magazines that Pete reads are real. People really did smoke cigarettes that way at the time. As for Pete, his family, and Kat, they are my inventions.

There are any number of memoirs of the time. Try *Wait Till Next Year* by Doris Kearns Goodwin, and *The Boy Detective: A New York Childhood* by Roger Rosenblatt.

Your loyal Giants fan,
Avi